SNIFFING OUT THE SPY

RIMMY LONDON

BOOKS &
GIFTS

Dedicated to all the best dogs.

Foreword

For a free holiday novella featuring Megan and Fred, type this link into your browser... https://dl.bookfunnel.com/kjrlku79ay

Find and follow Rimmy at her favorite places, including Bookbub, Facebook, and Amazon. See you there!

Chapter One

Megan Henny had to admit she'd always been a bit of a hippie. She considered this as she straightened tangled necklaces on the new countertop display. They'd been popular with tourists from the moment she put them out in her boardwalk shop, and that made her hippie heart happy. The teal stones were most popular, but she favored the tiny amber gems, and the way light would shine through, causing them to glow. There were three around her neck, draped in a subtle v and copycatting the neckline of her white lace tank. They went well with her auburn hair and green eyes.

Desmond's rather glum teenage voice pulled her from her thoughts. He was the grandson of a cheerful and very English friend who owned the bookshop only a few doors down. Working as her assistant, he was helping a customer return a beautiful blue scooter. His shaggy black hair hung in his face most days, and today was no exception. It seemed his vision was mostly obstructed by the mass of keratin, but if it was, he didn't show it. The customer walked out of the shop, and Megan looked over the scooter quickly, assuring there was no damage. Desmond always filled out a damage report when needed, but still... there was the question of his hair.

A squeal of tires from outside had Megan spinning around. She braced for the inevitable collision of metal on metal. But there was only a *thump-bump-squeal*. She rushed to the doorway to see a young couple stepping off one of her blue scooters, having collided with a small sedan. She hurried outside, grateful they hadn't met with a truck or bus.

Both the man and woman appeared okay, and Megan sighed with relief. Although the same could not be said for her scooter. It was severely crumpled.

"Oh man, we're all right!" The man was in swim trunks, and the woman sported a black bikini. She smacked him on the arm. "Are you insane?" she shouted with a shaky voice. "Watch where you're going!"

A gray-haired woman stepped out from the driver's side with a look of terror on her face. "I'm so sorry," she said in quiet shock. "There was no time to stop. You know you have a yield sign when coming from that direction."

The man laughed, and Megan started. What exactly did he find funny? She assumed it to be nervous laughter and caught up to them as quickly as she could.

"Are you both okay?" She looked at the man first. His cheeks were flushed, and his eyes watery and unfocused. "I'm sorry." She held his arm and waited for his focus to turn to her. He still had a ridiculous smile on his face, as if he'd done something impressive. "Are you drunk?" But by then, Megan didn't even need to ask. She could smell that he was.

The girl charged forward. Megan jumped out of the way as she slapped him again, this time so hard it echoed through the boardwalk. The man flinched and faced her quickly, and Megan took a hasty step between them. "Hold on, you two,"

"You're drunk, Daniel, admit it!" The woman's voice was shrill with panic. "You raging idiot!" Tears showed in her opaque brown eyes as she continued to scream. "We're done for good this time, so wipe that stupid smile off your dim face. I'm leaving!" She spun around in her bikini and sandals, charging away with more intimidation than Megan would have thought possible in such scanty clothing. With a deep breath, she turned back to the man. He was watching the girl but didn't seem to have caught everything that was said.

"Sorry 'bout the scooter." He turned to Megan. "We signed a waiver, though, right?"

"Yes, but waivers don't exactly buy me a new scooter."

"Nah, but insurance does." He grinned, walking with her as she towed the scooter out of the street. She pushed the kickstand forward, glad it was still functioning, and went to talk to the woman in the sedan. Collecting her information quickly, she apologized and assured the woman it wasn't her fault. But when she turned back, the man named Daniel was gone.

She scanned the boardwalk and caught sight of Fred, her gray and black dappled Great Dane, trotting down the wooden planks of the walkway. His long legs gave him the advantage of standing out against the two-legged crowd around him. He sniffed the air and then turned and faced the café, sitting with a plop. He glanced at Megan and then back to the eatery.

"Well, I guess I know where he went," Megan mumbled as she walked the scooter around the side of her shop. She caught Desmond's gaze from inside. "Keep an eye on things," she said. He only flicked his head up in reply, but she'd come to know that was teenager code for *yes*.

She sighed, her heart feeling heavy. Behind her shop was another scooter, a twisted mass of metal, almost completely lost. The unfortunate driver of that one had ended up with a broken leg. She was glad it hadn't been worse but also devastated that she was down two scooters. In a shop as small as hers, that was a big deal.

Her dreams of living the slow, easy seaside life she'd enjoyed as a child remained far out of reach. She thought back to the promise she made to her terminally ill friend Allie and wondered if she'd let herself get too caught up in unrealistic dreaming. Maybe she needed to face the fact that life wasn't really made to enjoy, but to live. To exist. To get by as well as you could.

She leaned against the sea-green shingles of her shop. The little building really was beautiful, with its rustic seaside look and oversized lampposts. But beautiful didn't pay the rent. The pine trees spread out behind the boardwalk were tall and had stood the tests of time. They'd lived a life a hundred times longer than hers. She gazed at the rich, healthy layers of growth around each trunk and the deep green pine needles dripping from every branch. They seemed to communicate directly to her heart, filling her with a hope she wasn't sure she should believe in.

But there was something about those noble life forms that spoke to her, telling her she wasn't wrong. That life was meant for everything. The good and the bad, the incredible and the challenging. She couldn't choose between one or the other; she could only wait for the next cycle to start.

She gazed down at the two ruined scooters, and pain tightened her chest as she faced the hard facts that she would have to close, at least temporarily. She couldn't keep going like this. Two crashes within such a short time of each other told her that the town wasn't ready for pleasure scooters. Not yet, anyway.

If she sold the scooters, that would make enough for her to purchase a small car. She needed one. Then maybe she could get a job close by and work until she came up with something that might be successful on the boardwalk. Something she could create that would live in countless childhood memories of visiting Seacrest, just as her trips to the picturesque Washington seaside town had lived in hers.

The sound of barking caught her attention. Fred was an intelligent dog, and she knew him well enough to know he didn't make noise just for the fun of it. She hurried back down to the boardwalk café where the large Great Dane stood in front of Daniel, blocking his exit from the building. Daniel held half a burger in one hand and yawned. "Outta my way, dog," he grumbled, kicking a foot out and then stumbling to the side.

"Excuse me, sir." Megan patted Fred's shoulder, and he retreated a step, giving her the lead. "I'll be sending you a bill for your portion of the damage to the scooter."

"Who are you?" he grumped, yawning a second time. He looked ready to pass out. With a sigh, Megan tapped his arm. "You'll remember tomorrow. Go back to your hotel and sleep it off."

Without another word, he ambled away, swaying a bit every few steps. Megan rubbed Fred's silky ears. "C'mon, boy."

She started back to the shop, feeling close to tears the nearer she got. Closing it was the only thing to do, but what now? She wasn't ready to give up and go back to nursing. It wasn't for her. She'd spent nine years in an emergency room in Seattle, living off very little sleep and caring to the point that it hurt. Separating herself from her patients was a skill she hadn't managed to develop, and it left her practically traumatized. Going back was not an option.

Her throat felt thick as she stepped inside the beautiful little shop, but there was a police officer standing at the counter. She hurried across the room, greeting him. He was familiar to her; she'd turned in a dark South Sea pearl necklace to him a couple of months earlier. The town had been in commotion for quite a while after learning that the builder for the newest affluent neighborhood had been smuggling jewelry under the foundations. But the museum he'd stolen from hadn't claimed the necklace, and so it had gone to the station until they could find the owner.

"Looks like these belong to you now." The officer handed her a long rectangular jewelry box with a smile. "No one claimed them, and any of the leads we followed went cold."

"I can't believe it." Megan looked down at the box in shock. "Are you sure?"

"Yes, ma'am," he said cheerfully with a dip of his head. "Thanks for your honesty."

She watched him leave, holding the box in her hand. Inside it was a strand of 84 South Sea pearls, glimmering black and shining like polished ebony. Retrieving her backpack from her office, she slipped the box inside and her arms through the straps of her bag. Desmond was wiping off the countertop. It made her proud anytime he did things without her specifically requesting they be done. She leaned against the counter next to him, looking out at the shop. It was nearing the end of the day, and the small room was empty. All the scooters had been returned, so there was no point in dragging it out further.

"I think we're going to have to close for a while, Desmond." She looked back at him, trying to smile, but mostly her lips just thinned. "I'm sorry. It's nearly the end of the season, and I don't have it in me to attempt a startup when there's only a few weeks of tourism left. I'd love to have you back as soon as I open again, but I'm not sure what kind of shop it'll be." She lifted an eyebrow. "Any ideas?"

"Uh..." He appeared to be thinking this information over in his head, turning it over like the slow spin of a cement truck. "Well, weed is pretty popular now. You could always open a cannabis shop."

"Huh." Megan wasn't sure how to respond to that, but it was the first time she'd seen Desmond look interested in something. She nodded back, trying to look like her wrinkled nose meant she was thinking about it. "Well, whatever I decide to do, I'll let your grandma know so you can get back to work as soon as possible."

"K. Thanks." He brushed a hand through his hair and wandered out of the shop, kicking the doorstop out of the way as he went. It swung shut, and Megan walked through the store slowly. She twisted the blinds and locked the front door, turning the small sign in the window to CLOSED.

Fred was sitting on his bed behind the counter with his ears perked up. He watched her, communicating that he knew full well she was doing something out of the ordinary.

When she lifted his leash from the hook on the wall, he leapt from his bed and scrambled down the slippery hallway to greet her at the back door. She clipped the leash onto his collar and took one last look at her crushed dreams before stepping outside.

Fred was now a professional at running alongside her bike through the woods. The trail was winding and hilly, but he kept up with ease. No more shooting across the path in front of her or stopping abruptly to sniff something and inadvertently hurling her from her bike. A chuckle found its way through her discouragement as she reminisced about her many prior face plants in the soft foliage of the forest.

Her home was one of only a few houses built in a remote part of the forest. None of the others were in view. In fact, she hadn't even known they were there until an untimely flash flood had prompted a rescue mission for all of them. It was how she'd met Santiago, although now there were rumors that he'd been arrested and accused of espionage. But it was impossible; it had to be a false report.

She smiled just thinking of him, a young man skirting

college and attempting to find meaning in his life. At least, that was what it looked like to Megan. If she were really being honest, she'd acknowledge the stark similarities between his plight and hers. She shook her head, refusing. He was close to ten years younger than her, after all. Even if he did have a silly crush on her, it was ridiculous. She'd finished school and had a career. Just because she was starting up again, it didn't mean she was lost in life. She knew exactly what she wanted.

With a sigh, she stepped off her bike and guided it up the porch steps, leaning it against the house. Her place was small but well kept. And what it lacked in accommodations, it more than made up for in views. Her entire living area was filled with deep, dark green pines and glimpses through the forest around her. There was remodeling yet to be done, especially since it had been abandoned by the contractor halfway through the job. But she could manage it on her own, especially now that she was closing the shop for a while. She'd have loads of time for the repairs to the siding and flooring and all the rest... hopefully.

But at least the fireplace was working. It was always the first thing she turned on, even before the lights. It glowed and flickered in the dark space, giving the illusion of warmth before she'd even felt its touch. Fred walked in a circle on the rug, directly in front of the fire, and settled down. Megan watched him, smiling. It was strange being a dog person when she'd spent most of her life being utterly afraid of them. How curious that she would end up with one of the largest dogs she'd ever seen.

She sat on the couch and faced the thoughts that were hovering around her like obnoxious visitors. They wouldn't leave until she gave them attention, and so she did. Her life was in an upheaval again, and she needed to make some decisions. Closing her shop temporarily was the right choice. She could feel it. Plus, she had no choice. But what to do next, she had no idea. There was already a book shop and a café, and next door to her was Crystal's handmade jewelry. What could Megan bring to the boardwalk that would complement them all without becoming competition?

Her phone rang. The number on the screen was unknown, which she would usually ignore. But out of curiosity, she answered it.

"Is this Megan Henny?"

She affirmed the question and listened through a strange explanation of why this very detail-oriented person was calling her out of the blue. He claimed to represent Mr. Santiago Fitch and said he was relaying a message from his client. To have it confirmed that Santiago was behind bars was shocking. She'd heard through various friends about his predicament and had assumed his name would be cleared in no time. That he'd been through the worst of it and would return to Seacrest. But now that the accusations were real, it had her asking herself what she really knew about him. It left a knot in her stomach to realize she knew practically nothing.

"He wishes to speak with you," the man stated.

"I'm sorry, what?" Megan sat up straighter on her couch.

"He was hoping you'd be able to make it out to the South Seattle Jail to visit with him. Is that a possibility?"

"Uh..." Megan hesitated, feeling uncomfortable with the idea. But then she thought back to the three days Santiago had spent trapped under the foundation of a house in the Edgewater Estates. He'd been trying to help her and was very nearly murdered for it. Megan could have come to his rescue then, but she made the mistake of assuming he'd left town. It was a decision that still sent chills up her spine. If she'd waited even one night more, it would have been a very different story.

Well, she didn't want to make that mistake again. Santiago was young and impulsive, but he was a good person who was clearly in trouble. This time, she was going to do what she could to help him. "Yes," she answered, finding it convenient that her schedule was suddenly clear. "I can come in a few days."

"Thank you. I'll email over the details. Have a good night."

"Thank y—"

"Goodbye."

Megan pulled the phone from her ear, glancing at the screen to see the call had ended. "Thank you."

So, now she was visiting Santiago in jail in Seattle? It was definitely a strange twist in her plans. And it had her wondering just why Santiago would want to meet with *her*. What could he possibly need? Comfort? Companionship? Because she'd been pretty clear with him that she wasn't looking for a relationship. Far from looking, she was recovering. After years of dating Jarron, followed by a sudden proposal, she'd realized it then. It was her catalyst, the moment she knew where she wanted her life to go. Or at least, where she *didn't* want it to. Her years ahead were hers alone, and she refused to lean on anyone else. But there was the fact that Santiago had basically invested in her business without her knowing, paying for the remodel... or at least, the start of it. Too bad the contractor was also a murderer.

She groaned, rubbing a hand across her face. Maybe he just wanted his money back. The son of Mark and Carolina Fitch, famed international jewelers, digging for money? That didn't make any sense, either. The more she turned it over in her head, the stranger it seemed. Of all the people he could contact, why would Santiago want to talk to her?

Chapter Two

Megan stood just outside *Marg's Books*. The shop had opened minutes earlier, and tourists, it seemed, had yet to wander in. Fred seemed lazier than usual in the morning, as if he wouldn't have minded another hour of sleep. But he wandered in when she did, sniffing happily as if he enjoyed the delightful cinnamon and cloves candles as much as she did. The shelves were carved like tree trunks and branches, and the lanterns hanging about the place made it feel magical. A very Secret-Garden-Meets-Harry-Potter feel. Margaret Thornton was a genius with how she put it together, but then she was completely in love with books, so it made sense.

"Hello, dear, hello!" Margaret rushed from the back of the store and past the suspense and science fiction aisles. "It's been too long." She wrapped Megan up in a squeeze. Her bouncy gray hair smelled of lilacs, and it made Megan smile.

She dropped Fred's leash and let him wander while they chatted. "Yes, it has," she said to Margaret. "How's your shop? It looks beautiful today with the cloud cover outside and the lanterns all aglow."

The room around them was more enchanting than she remembered, but when her eyes wandered back to Margaret, there was a very uncustomary glower on the sprightly woman's face. She was staring out the window of the shop, and Megan turned around to see a lineup of various trucks in the parking lot, adjacent to the boardwalk and next to the beach. A few people had already gathered in front of the *Coffee Hut*.

Margaret finally pulled her gaze from the scene outside and blinked back at Megan. "I'm sorry, what?"

"Is something wrong?" Megan ventured.

"Oh, no. Nonsense." Margaret trudged back through the fantasy aisle and began organizing papers behind the counter. "I guess I've just been busier than usual, is all."

"Uh-huh." Megan turned around to gaze across the empty store again. When she faced Margaret, the older woman let her arms drop to her sides.

"Well yes, then, if you must know. I've been empty all week! Those food trucks are going to have us all out of business. And here the mayor has to go and create a lot of buzz over it, claiming it's going to be the most festive summer's end ever! A blubbering blowhard is what he is. I can't hardly sell my tea over there, and no one is coming in for books over here. So how, exactly, is this such a grand thing?"

"Wait, you've got a booth?" Megan asked, impressed.

"A *truck*, dear." Margaret corrected, always insistent on the most proper word in every sentence.

Megan smiled. "Well, that's great. You just need a bit of promotion or something."

"Figgles," Margaret grouched. "No one wants tea. They're all over there guzzling coffee like camels intending to walk the Sahara."

"Well." Megan glanced back at the *Coffee Hut* to see it had opened its window, and the line had more than tripled. "Uh, maybe they'll get tired of coffee after a while and want something a little more soothing." She turned back to Margaret and held in a laugh at the height of her eyebrows. It was impressive.

"Have you ever heard a coffee drinker say they were tired of coffee? Ever?" Margaret swished her hand through the air in front of them. "But no matter, I apologize for being such a whiney Winny. Here you come to say hello, and I fill your ear with rubbish. Was there something you wanted to talk about, hun?"

"Oh, no, it's fine." Megan glanced back at the trucks to see a few more had opened, and tourists were buzzing around between them like bees in a flower field. It was definitely popular. But then she spotted a small truck along the side of the culinary curve. The *Tea Time* sign was adorable, lit up with a strand of oversized globe lights and two picnic tables with bright yellow umbrellas. Definitely a sunny idea. She chewed her lip, wondering how they could turn the tables and get Margaret's truck selling.

"Then, you just came in to say hello?"

Margaret's question had her remembering why she'd come in. Not that she could forget for very long; it was like an elephant plunked right atop her head.

"I did come to say hello, but there was something else I wanted to ask you." She couldn't stop the somber expression from surfacing on her face.

The change in Margaret's demeanor was immediate. She set down the notebook and pen she was holding and leaned over the counter. "Yes?" the older woman inquired.

Megan knew Margaret had spun a few tales just in the short time she'd known her. Half the store owners on the boardwalk now thought Megan was some kind of super sleuth when really she'd only stumbled across a stolen necklace. In truth, everything she'd solved had been because of Fred. But

Margaret knew how to talk, and if anyone had heard about Santiago, it would be her.

"I, uh..." Megan took a steadying breath. "I wanted to ask about Santiago."

Margaret nodded. "I thought so, dear. I thought so. He is in a bit of trouble, that one. I feel for him because I know he's got such goodness. But there's also a lot that he keeps hidden, and that's the part that worries me."

Megan tried to veer the conversation away from the conspiracy theory direction it seemed to be headed. "I was hoping you'd be able to tell me what you've heard about him. Why he's in trouble and all that. I don't know much, but I might get the chance to speak with him before too long and—"

"Oh, will you?" Margaret's blue eyes widened.

"I think so," Megan said, wishing she'd kept quiet. The attorney hadn't exactly said he wanted it kept quiet, but wasn't that always implied with attorneys? "It's sort of confidential," she whispered.

"Of course, dear." Margaret looked around the room, even though a customer had yet to enter. "I've heard his own parents started the investigation." She began. "They've accused him of corporate espionage, which is a pretty hefty accusation. Especially from his own family, poor thing."

"I agree. That's horrible." Megan had been hoping there was some mishap with communication, and it was all a big mistake. A different guy or a different family, maybe. But that didn't seem likely.

"Now," Margaret began, both hands gesturing as she spoke, "I hear he was still working for the company, even after he moved to Seacrest. That might have been part of the problem. If he was trying to steal away clients from his parents and branch off to his own business?" She tilted her head in thought. "Or possibly he was working for them remotely and just not taking in a profit. Maybe he didn't want anyone knowing where he was, so he forfeited the commissions for now. Hmm." She rubbed her chin, where there were a few stubby white whiskers. "If that were the case, maybe this whole investigation was just a ruse, so they could simply find him. Now *that* would be an interesting twist."

Megan sighed, feeling overloaded with possibilities. "I guess I'll just have to wait and see what happens."

The bell jingled. They both stood and glanced at the front of the room to see three teenage girls wander in. They were absorbed in their conversation and instantly attracted to the fantasy aisle where they giggled incessantly.

Margaret smiled a twinkly smile, clearly enjoying the patronage. "You have a wonderful day, Megan. Please let me know what you hear. If you speak to him, tell him we all miss having him around. He's such a cheerful personality."

"I agree. Bye, Margaret." Megan walked through the store and patted her leg with one hand as she walked, signaling Fred. His head lifted from where he'd curled up on the floor, and he followed her out, dragging his leash with him. She hardly had need of it anymore, but there were warning signs that dogs needed to be on a leash. And really, Fred *had* run off a time or two, so the leash stayed. She picked it up off the ground and decided to check out the parking lot vendors.

Fred definitely seemed more engaged. His head was lifted high and regal, swiveling from the sounds of sizzling bacon at the *Burger Joint* to the popping caramel corn at the *Kettle Corral.* Sweet and savory smells floated around them, wafting by with each shift in the breeze. Every truck had business that Megan could see. Everyone except for Margaret's.

She walked up to the window to spot Desmond kicked back on a stool. He was leaning against the wall with two wooden legs of the stool tilted off the ground precariously, in danger of falling with each second that passed. He pushed buttons on his phone, clearly engaged in a game, and didn't even notice Megan was there. "Hey, Desmond," she said.

He jumped and the legs of the chair slid from under him, landing him hard on the floor. With his phone still gripped tight in his hands, he only looked mildly stunned. He found Megan a moment later, and an ever so subtle look of aware-ness appeared on his features. At least, from what could be seen under his hair. "Oh hey, Megan." He scrambled up awkwardly, lifting the stool onto its feet again. "You want some tea?"

And even with service like this, no one was lining up for tea? Megan cleared her throat, chiding herself. "Why not?" she asked. "I'll try the lemon chamomile with honey, please."

"Oh." Desmond didn't look like he had expected her answer, but he got to work. His hands bumped and thumped through the task of separating a Styrofoam cup from its stack. He filled it with steaming water and added two bags and a hefty squeeze of honey before adding a stirring straw. "Five dollars, please."

She handed him the money, all the while deliberating on what could be done to get people coming to the forgotten little tea truck.

"Have a good'n." Desmond *thunked* against the back wall as he tilted on the stool again, thumbs flying atop the screen of his cell phone.

Megan savored the hot, sweet drink, staring back at Desmond. He had potential in there, somewhere. One of these days, she'd find a way to drag it out of him.

But today, she already knew what she had to do. If she planned to travel to Seattle, and also planned to discontinue her scooter rentals, it was only reasonable that selling the scooters to pay for a car was the way to go. Selling the pearls had been her first thought, but there was something about them that had her hesitating. Every time she considered it, she would pull them from the box and gaze into their shimmering, inky cores... and return them to her backpack. They might be in her possession, but for reasons she couldn't define, she knew they weren't hers.

She'd have to rely on the scooters.

It didn't take long to find an ecstatic online buyer, and the scooters sold in less than a day. The man dropped everything and drove four hours to pick them up. It left her wishing she would have raised the price just a bit. But it was too late now. She gazed over the $12,000 in her bank account. She needed gas money, food for her and Fred, and a little cushion to invest in whatever shop she wanted to open next. With a sigh, she divided the money in half and transferred one sum into savings. The rest was all she had for a car. A *reliable* car that could make it to Seattle and back... preferably more than once.

The little car dealership in Seacrest was her only hope, since Santiago's attorney was expecting her in Seattle the next day. She looked across the dozen dusty, rusty clunkers and then back at Fred. No one had come out of the office doors yet, for which she was grateful. She hurried through the cars, hoping to make a quick decision. Fred sniffed at a little red hatchback, but the back window looked like a brick had been lugged through it. She leaned in and a dry laugh escaped her lips. "Look at that, Fred. There's a brick on the backseat."

She hurried past a beastly Cadillac, even though she could hear her friend Allie's voice in her head.

But the backseat is literally a couch, and you'd survive a crash with anything!

She smiled and passed two small pickup trucks and a minivan. There was a plain white Volkswagen that looked like it would probably run. She kept that one logged in her mind and browsed a rusty maroon sedan and a tiny two door Civic.

"Hello!" boomed a voice behind her, and she gasped, nearly jumping out of her shoes. "Welcome to Cam's Car Lot!" The man was tall and thick, and he walked as fast as he talked. "We've got a lot of really great cars right now, so you don't want to miss out. What exactly are you looking for, miss?" He glanced at Fred and took a small step back.

"Er..." Megan hesitated. "I'm not sure. I just need something reliable that isn't too much. Does this one run well?" She pointed to the white Volkswagen.

"Yes, absolutely! Everything on the lot runs well." He winked at her. "Now, running well for how long is the question." A hearty laugh shook through him, and he walked past the white car, the minivan, and the trucks. Megan trailed behind him, wondering if he would just be showing her the one he wanted off the lot first.

"I'll be heading to Seattle tomorrow," she added. "So, I need something that can at least make the trip and hopefully will be able to run for a few years. It doesn't have to be pretty." She glanced around again, realizing she could have left that last part off since it applied to every single vehicle around them.

"This one here would do the trick." He stopped at the Cadillac, and Megan cringed a little as he continued, "It runs well, is safe for traveling long distances, and would have plenty of room for your four-legged friend, here." He nodded at Fred.

She looked past the Cadillac to the red hatchback. Now that she saw it from the other direction, it was actually pretty cute. It had a nice shape, and the paint wasn't rusted anywhere that she could see. Plus, it would be easy to lay down the backseat and open up the hatch for Fred to go in and out.

"What about this little one?" She gestured to the car. "The only problem is the back window. I would need that repaired, and I don't know if there'd be time since I have to leave tomorrow."

"Huh," He glanced back at Fred. "You sure you want that one? Your dog is pretty large."

"I'd put the backseat down." She smiled, feeling better and better about it. Fred even wandered over to the car and wagged his tail. Of course, there were a few chips that someone had spilled on the ground. But she told herself, as he munched on the newfound treats, that it meant he liked the car too. More and more, it felt like the one. "How much is it?"

"Oh, that one's seven thousand." He shook his head solemnly. "What's your budget?"

Megan was eyeing him as best she could, pulling from her years of experience as a nurse, asking people to take their medications. It seemed to be working as he stretched his collar with one hand. "C'mon," she urged. "You can take that price down. There's a brick literally in the back seat!"

"Well, yes. That's unfortunate." His slicked black hair glimmered in the lamppost lighting as he turned from her to the car and back. "Just happened yesterday and I haven't had a chance to clean it up."

"Let me get it off your hands for five thousand and your guys can work your magic and repair the back window for me. I can have it off your lot tonight." She held her breath, hoping he would say yes. Suddenly, more than anything, she needed this car. It was the one. She watched his every move as his eyes surveyed the dusty, broken vehicle and then glanced back at her quickly before reverting to his own feet.

"Hmm," he said, "lemme see what the boss says about that."

Ugh, the boss. She knew perfectly well there was no boss.

The office looked completely deserted with zero signs of life. But she wanted to stay on his good side, so she cheerfully agreed and tried to look relaxed and uncommitted as he walked back to the office.

"This is the one, Fred," she whispered. He was still sniffing around, trying to find another chip. "We're gonna drive to Seattle and find a way to clear Santiago's name."

"I'm sorry, ma'am."

She spun around, surprised he had returned so quickly.

His lips were downturned, and he appeared genuinely disheartened.

Dang, he's good.

"We can't go down on the price. It's already priced to sell."

Megan made a point of looking around the empty lot. "Yes, but it hasn't sold. How long has it been here?"

"I apologize—"

"Never mind, I'll go someplace else." She turned and started walking away, her heart pounding. She knew perfectly well she could go up to the six thousand she had in her pocket, but what then? What if there were extra fees? What if they wanted her to pay for the window? No, she couldn't budge. But as she made it to the sidewalk and the distance between her and the car lot grew, she wondered if she'd made a mistake.

"Wait a minute, ma'am!"

A wicked grin spread the length of her face. *Winner, winner, chicken dinner.*

Chapter Three

Fred looked back at her with his nose caked in dirt. His eyes were teasing, not anywhere near sorry.

"Now Fred," she began, trying not to smile when his ears lifted at his name. "I thought we'd gotten over this habit. It needs to stop, especially when we're talking about my floor." With a dramatic sweep of her hand, she pointed out the dirt prints through the kitchen where he'd walked before she realized what a dirt-covered state he was in. His eyes looked curious for half a second before he sat and scratched at his ear.

"And after I clean up this mess, we're going to have to give you a bath." His reaction was immediate, bouncing from the floor like he'd been electrocuted. His tail whipped back and forth in a blur of excitement. Megan rolled her eyes to the sky. It was basically the opposite of a punishment for him. If only she could find something he didn't completely love.

She leaned over him and tapped his dirty nose playfully. "Now no more digging, okay? You're gonna excavate the foundation if you keep it up."

He froze for a moment and then sneezed, flapping his

ears and spraying her with a face-full of dirt. "Ugh, Fred! Bleh." She wiped at her face, laughing. "When is it your turn to have a consequence or two?"

After glancing at the clock, she sighed and got to work, wiping Fred's paws enough not to leave tracks and then starting on the floor. The realization that she was going back to Seattle in less than twelve hours began to sink in a little more. She hadn't fully thought out the possibility of seeing her ex or her parents. Not that she didn't want to see her family, but they insisted on being so critical of her decision to dump Jarron. Too bad they never got the chance to see just how dark his manipulative side was. They only saw the polished, smooth as silk, and so very clever version. The perfect Jarron.

With the floor clean, she grabbed Fred's collar and led him to the bathroom. Closing the door, she went through her emergency dog bath checklist. It had been honed after many unsuccessful attempts, starting with the closed door. Next was towels on the floor. Check. Extra towels hanging in arm's reach of the tub, check. More towels folded on the counter, double check.

She turned on the faucet, peering back at Fred while she added some dog shampoo to the water. He sat like an angel on the rug. But she knew better. "Stay," she warned, giving him her serious face. It was the same face she'd used on the car salesman, and hopefully, it worked on dogs. He shook out his coat and yawned. "We're bathing you civilized-like this time," she continued in her most soothing voice. "No jumping, no splashing, no tromping, or stomping... got it?"

Thirty minutes later, with several layers of soaked clothing hanging from the shower rod, she squeezed her hair into the tub. Wrapped in the last available towel, she sat with her back against the tub and surveyed the scene. Bubbles were crowded at the edge of the many towels laid across the floor.

They were all in varying stages of wetness, with most being as drenched through as Megan was. Exhaustion had sunk clear to her bones, especially when she thought about packing for the next day. All she wanted to do was crawl into bed and sleep for ten hours at least.

But Fred was clean, and he was dry. A sound came from the kitchen that she eventually narrowed down to Fred's tail smacking against the kitchen cabinets.

And apparently, he was hungry.

He'd obviously come up with a new way to ask for his dinner after he learned that scratching on the floor wasn't allowed. Before that, he learned about not scratching at the door. And before that was barking, and then putting his front paws up on the counter... and also grabbing the bag of dog food with his teeth to drag it across the floor. Each time, he learned very quickly what not to do, but it seemed he came up with a new terrible idea almost immediately.

Thwap. Thwap. Thwap.

The sound vibrated the wood cabinets slightly, as if it were something close to actual music. It really was the least annoying of his tactics so far, but that didn't mean it was pleasant. After listening to a few more drum beats of his tail, Megan struggled up from the bathroom floor and got dressed into some wonderfully dry clothes.

"I'm coming, Fred." Her voice seemed to calm him, and the tail strikes stopped. She ran her fingers through her towel-dried hair, enjoying the manageable length. It hung just past her shoulders, dark strands of ginger.

Jarron has always wanted her to keep it long, even after she'd wanted to cut it multiple times. But long was sexy, so it stayed. The second she'd broken off their relationship, she'd taken a pair of scissors to it. The length was too short; she realized it almost immediately, but she didn't care. It was also freedom. Now that it had grown a few inches, it was perfect.

Enough to dress up with waves and still keep the tangles away.

She went to the kitchen and shook some food into Fred's dish, and he sat, looking up at her until she was finished. He always seemed a bit unsure if the food was actually for him or not. It made her sad to picture how long he'd been a stray, out stealing scraps and dodging angry victims of his hunger. When Megan thought about it, he really had been terribly skinny when she first saw him. She patted his head encouragingly. "Go on, it's all yours." He proceeded to wolf it down, knocking dozens of pieces of kibble out of the bowl and onto the floor.

The evening was getting late, with darkness out her windows and the ticking of the clock becoming more noticeable, as it seemed to be every night. She looked at the time winding by and went to her room to drag her suitcase out from under her bed. It was a relief to have a car, and she felt a sudden surge of excitement at the thought of a road trip.

☙❧

THE DRIVE WAS LONGER THAN SHE'D EXPECTED.

"FRED, FOR THE LAST TIME, STAY ON YOUR SIDE."
  "Down, boy,"
  "Sit."
  "Can you breathe out the window, please?"
  "Eww, Fred, again?!"
  "No drool for me, thanks."
  "Fred!"

. . .

HER NERVES WERE A LITTLE FRAZZLED AFTER THREE HOURS, but she figured the South Seattle Jail wasn't the type of place she needed to be glamoured up for, anyway. Still, she pulled out her purse and searched for her lip gloss.

"Fred, you really are good company," she said, glancing down at where he was curled up on the passenger seat. He'd refused to lay in the back, and she hadn't really been up for a fight about it. So, he'd been plunked down next to her the whole time. But when he accidentally pushed the gear shift into neutral as she was on the last stretch of freeway, she'd snapped at him. Now he was pouting and refused to look at her.

"You are," she repeated, running her hand down his back. His coat had filled in and was sleek and shiny, a vast improvement from the patchy, dry mess it had been before. She scratched his favorite spot between his shoulder blades, and he lifted his head, tipping his nose to the ceiling. He couldn't help but enjoy a good scratch.

"Do you forgive me? I'm sorry I shouted when you almost had us smashed by the semi behind us, who was going much too fast and probably would only feel a small bump if our car went under all of its eighteen tires."

Fred turned and looked back at her. He pushed off the seat cushion suddenly to bless her face with his giant tongue.

"Aaand I was afraid of that." She wiped her face quickly and painted on some lip gloss. "It'll have to do." Her voice felt shaky, and her hands matched. She took a slow deep breath. Fred commenced panting and stared out the window that was nearly impossible to see through anymore. Slobber and paw prints had left it quite the mess.

"The attorney said I could bring you inside, and he agreed to keep you in his office. But I told him you'd be a good boy." She waited for him to acknowledge her. "Fred?"

He turned his head, looking much too aware of what she was saying.

"You'll be a good boy, right, Fred?"

His responded with a burp.

"Oh boy." Megan stepped out of the car. The day was pleasant, perhaps a little chilly, but it was Seattle, after all. She grew up in the chill. At least it wasn't raining... yet. There were a few clouds on the horizon that looked like they wanted to cause some trouble. Fred was bursting with energy after sitting in a car for so long. The second she clipped his leash on, he circled her three times, nearly toppling her over. But she'd parked at the back of the lot in order to give him a small walk on the way in. Not much, but hopefully enough.

When they entered, all eyes were on Fred. Megan quickly surmised that the attorney's offer of dog sitting wasn't something that happened every day. Or possibly ever. His collar jangling and claws clicking on the cheap vinyl flooring caught everyone's attention who hadn't already been staring. She felt a little relieved when she made it to the desk in front. A woman as excited as rock stared back at her with an expression equally as cheerful, but there was no time for an introduction.

"Ms. Henny!" A voice called out from a much too skinny hall. It likely hailed to the 70s when she assumed the building was constructed. She turned to see the man whose name she wished she knew. He'd introduced himself in the phone call, but it seemed like years ago. All she remembered was the attorney part.

"Hello, sir." She held her hand out, taking a quick appraisal of him as he approached. He seemed exceptionally young with a gorgeous smile and the whitest teeth she'd ever seen. His skin was a rich and dark, and his hair hung down in something close to braids but a little different. She felt herself blushing as they shook hands, trying not to stare but not wanting to look at the floor, either.

"I'm sorry, Mr. Yost had to step out."

Mr. Yost! That was his name.

She tried to force her flushed cheeks to cool. "Oh, uh, no problem. Are you his assistant?"

He shook his head pleasantly, making the bundle of strands on top tumble around just a bit. "No, I'm Derek Montel, a resident attorney here. Just learning what I can from the master." He winked. "Here, I'll take you to his office. Right this way, follow me."

Still flustered, Megan couldn't think of anything to say. So she followed, taking a quick stock of the building. The walls and ceiling were all the same dingy yellow color that she had to assume used to be white many years ago. Everything smelled of stale coffee and asbestos.

"Here we are," Derek said.

He held the door for her, and she walked through, squeezing a little to allow for Fred as he insisted on entering at the exact moment as her. The office was nice. It even smelled newer compared to the rest of the building and looked slightly refurbished. The walls were packed with bookshelves, but in a good way. No overcrowding or stacking, and the many legal volumes were displayed with pride, next to various interesting trophies and awards.

"I like your dog," Derek said as he closed the door. "He's big."

Megan smiled. "Yes, he really is. I was actually terrified of him at first..." She paused at the way Derek walked cautiously toward her.

"I'm sorry we couldn't be more forward with you over the phone," he whispered. "We'll have to communicate quietly in here. Information has been leaked recently, and we're still unsure of how. I apologize."

"Oh," Megan whispered, "I actually have no idea why Santiago wants to meet with me. We're friends, but I only just met him a few months ago, and he's been out of town for a lot of that time."

"Yes, I understand." Derek nodded. "I attended my first semester of college with Santiago, you know. But he hasn't been able to speak freely with us since we realized someone was leaking information. We've searched for a bug but so far haven't found anything."

They sat down on the couch, with Fred sitting next to them and Megan trying to make sense of things. "So, Derek," she whispered. He glanced up, poised on her next words. She tried to keep her thoughts together. "What exactly has Santiago been accused of? And are his parents really the ones who accused him?"

"Yes, that's right," he whispered, nodding. "I'm a little surprised you didn't know the details. I thought Yost had told you at least that much. Here, let me fill you in."

He pulled out his phone and swiped through a few screens packed with apps. So many icons, Megan would bet he ran his life with his phone. There was a money symbol, a grocery bag, a scorpion, a car. The screen was loaded with apps.

"Here we are." His voice was very quiet. He clicked on an icon of a pen and paper and looked up at her. "They did accuse him, but even they weren't sure of the details. They just want him investigated. Things have been shaky between the family since his brother basically embezzled millions from the company and disappeared. Looks like they isolated Santiago after this, leaving him in a high position in the company but also limiting what he had access to." He glanced down at his phone, scrolling through pages of text.

Fred leaned in, sniffing Derek's phone. "Hey, doggie." He patted the canine's head without looking up. "Ah, here we go. Santiago didn't attend the most recent gala his parents hosted, which was a pretty big deal. A slap in the face. I assure you, they noticed big time. And while he claims he just wanted to make a statement and get their attention, he didn't expect their reaction. They immediately dug into his accounts of two world renowned jewelers, one in Switzerland and one in France. Both had transactions that couldn't be tracked after the point they were sold to the company, and then they effectively vanish."

Megan felt her stomach twisting. "So, he *was* stealing from them?"

"No, he wasn't." Derek shook his head. "He claims the pieces were fakes and had been reproduced. He wanted to dig into the people directly involved in the transportation of the pieces and track down where the deception might be coming from. But before he had the chance, his parents had him thrown in here." He leaned back with a somber face. "And now he's asking for you, Ms. Henny."

"I have no idea why." Megan rubbed her hand on Fred's coat, trying to calm her nerves.

Derek stood. "Well, let's go find out."

Without a leash in her hands, Megan wasn't quite sure what to do with herself. She rubbed her hands together, and after noticing how sweaty her palms were, she rubbed them on her jeans. She was directed to a room constructed of cinder blocks and painted white. A row of cubicles stretched from wall to wall, with no access to the other side. A plexiglass panel separated them with laminate wood sheets on either side of each booth for privacy.

Contrary to what she thought, there were no phone receivers, just circular vents in the middle of the plexiglass to speak through. She rubbed her hands together, feeling her heart pound. What if there was some mistake, and Santiago had meant to ask for someone else? What if he just wanted to blame her for bringing all the media attention to Seacrest when he'd only wanted to be left alone? She nearly fled the room, but the inmate door opened. Five individuals were led through, each in a green jumpsuit and each walking slowly and carefully. Santiago's hair stood out the most, tied back in a ponytail, the golden-brown waves trailed past his shoulders. His olive and honey skin still looked sun-kissed, and his eyes were a bright sea-green even with the obnoxious fluorescent lighting. Each prisoner sat down, but no one spoke.

"You have twenty minutes." The guard's voice boomed across the enclosed space. He was big and a tad portly but obviously very capable of keeping the peace in any manner he might choose.

Santiago leaned forward immediately, speaking within inches of the vent. "Thank you so much for coming, Megan. You don't know how good it is to see you." His eyes were pained. "I'm sorry to have you see me like this, but I just... I don't know where to start."

Megan's heart was racing, a feeling of anguish nearly crushing her. He didn't belong in that jumpsuit being guarded like an animal. "I'm happy to come, really." Her throat seized up, and she swallowed hard. "I just keep thinking if all those reporters hadn't come to Seacrest—"

"No, don't say that." He shook his head, losing a strand of hair from his ponytail. It trailed down the side of his face. "None of this is your fault." He glanced back at the guard, who instantly bristled, and then turned back to Megan. "Can I just talk to you for a moment? I want to tell you what you mean to me."

Megan's heart rate picked up speed. This was not what she expected at all. But she leaned forward and gave her permission for him to continue.

Instantly he was off, rattling away and talking about their time together, and Seacrest, and her shop. Everything was mixed together, but it still managed to make her cry. She brushed a tear away just as everything changed. Suddenly he sounded incoherent, or drugged, or... she squinted, trying to make sense of his words.

"...please don't always be so extremely careful. It's not you. Your smile will and can be with me in times of danger. If I follow your example, the world will just rope us together behind me. Building Edgewater and even to my family the storms and beach are always beneath."

"Time's up, say your goodbye's."

Megan jumped, glancing over at the guard who somehow seemed to know every time she was going to look at him. He stared back with so little emotion he could have been a statue. She turned back to Santiago, thoroughly confused. He was making no sense. But her time was up, so what else could she say? Leaning in, she looked into his eyes as she spoke. "I hope we can see each other again soon, Santiago."

He leaned close, their faces inches apart. "Trace," he said quietly.

Megan froze, staring back at him with her lips parted, trying to see past his expression to determine if he'd lost his mind. She lifted her hand in a small wave and left the room. As she walked quietly with the other civilians, trailing behind a guard whose steps echoed, she knew that Santiago wasn't crazy. He was smart and caring. So if he went to the trouble of asking her to drive three hours to come see him, then took up their twenty minutes together by speaking gibberish, she could only conclude one thing.

He was speaking to her in code.

Chapter Four

"Hello Ms. Henny, I'm Clive Yost."

A tall man with gel-slicked hair and severe blue eyes shook her hand. Megan's head was still spinning, trying to dissect Santiago's words, but she managed a brief smile. "Hello."

The office was slightly ransacked, the contents of a few of the nicely organized shelves now strewn about. Fred was scrambling around, and Derek looked completely disheveled, with his face tinted with sweat.

But Mr. Yost didn't bat an eye. "I apologize I wasn't here earlier when you arrived. We spoke on the phone a few days ago," he said, releasing her hand.

His manner was very different from Derek's; the way he domineered the conversation with fierce politeness was intimidating. She could see why he was such a successful lawyer, as it wasn't difficult to imagine his friendliness changing at a shift in the wind. Or maybe it was just that Derek looked so completely normal the way he was frantically trying to untangle Fred's leash from the leg of his chair.

"Here." She knelt down, trying to help. Finally, she just

unclipped the leash and held onto Fred's collar while Derek slipped the knotted leash off the chair leg and handed it to her. He glanced quickly at Mr. Yost and began cleaning up books in a rush.

"Just to let you know"—Mr. Yost ignored the chaos completely as Megan reattached the leash—"we've had the room purged of any listening devices, so we can speak comfortably now. Also, you're not required to relay any of your conversation with Santiago to me."

Mr. Yost walked briskly to his desk and sat down at a sleek leather chair. "I will be speaking with him later today, though, if there's anything you would like me to ask him or relay to him?" He pulled out a notepad, poised.

"Er..." Megan hesitated, pulling a bit on the leash until Fred sat down. If Santiago's attorneys were so accessible to him, why wouldn't he tell them the strange message instead of her? Surely, they were clever and... accredited. If he chose to speak only to her, she had to assume the message was hers alone. She took a moment to sit down before replying, "Actually, Mr. Yost." She clasped her hands together instead of crossing them, intending to portray openness. "I would appreciate it if you could let him know how glad I am that we got to speak. If he needs me again, tell him just to ask, and I'm happy to drive out."

"Of course." He scribbled on the pad and flipped it over, dropping his pen to the desk. With a quick nod, he stood from his chair. "If that's all—"

"Can I ask you," Megan interrupted.

"Yes?" Mr. Yost paused and lowered back into his chair with a respectful look of concern. All he had to do was flinch, and it would be a formidable stare.

Megan cleared her throat. "I'm just wondering what Santiago is accused of. Derek told me a little, but what does Santiago have to say about it? He, uh, didn't have time to tell me very much, so I was hoping you could clear it up for me."

"Ah, I'm sorry about that." He glanced at Derek, who now sat quietly along the side of the room, pressing buttons on a handheld tablet.

The resident attorney looked up suddenly, as if sensing a change in the air. "I need to speak with the staff about your schedule over the next few days," he said quickly, standing. He cast a weary eye at Fred and then left the room.

"Thank you," Mr. Yost said, waiting until the door had closed behind him. He swiveled his chair, facing Megan again. "Now, Ms. Henny, there's a lot I am not at liberty to speak about."

"Yes. I fully respect that," Megan assured him.

"Thank you." He pressed his fingertips together, with his elbows resting on the desk. "Santiago negotiates with two jewelers. One in Switzerland and one in France." His eyes flickered up to hers. "This is public knowledge."

"Yes," she nodded, encouraging him to continue.

"His family is accusing him of espionage, yes." His eyes were focused on the bookcase, and they slowly found their way back to her. "But I'm also looking into a man he was working with. This man placed an order request nearly a year ago, according to Mr. Fitch, but the request was never filled."

He must have noticed the flecks of confusion on Megan's face as she tried to decide what that might mean.

"In other words, the client asked Mr. Fitch to find him a specific piece of jewelry, and Mr. Fitch couldn't locate it. A strange request, but one I cannot share with you at this time."

"I see." Megan's curiosity was pricked, imagining what elusive jewel Santiago might have been looking for and feeling a little downhearted that he never shared this information with her. The college dropout and vagabond image he'd portrayed was quickly fading away into something more complex. "So, how would that connect to his parents' accusations?"

"I'm not sure that it does." Mr. Yost stood from his chair and began to walk the length of the room, pacing in front of the bookcase. His suit was crisp and perfectly tailored, adding to his professionalism. Megan couldn't help but admire it as he walked.

"You see, when a particular jade bracelet passed through Santiago's hands, intended for a new client, he discovered a tiny air bubble on one side." He stopped pacing and turned to Megan. "Which told him the jade wasn't authentic. After that incident, he fired his appraiser and began authenticating everything himself... and what he found was shocking." He returned to his seat.

Fred yawned and lay down, and Megan suddenly felt herself eager to yawn. She stifled it as best as she could. Thankfully, Mr. Yost didn't seem to notice.

"Nearly half of the items weren't authentic. Mr. Fitch wanted to find the one responsible, claiming someone was faking authentic pieces, replicating them, and selling the originals on the side. He tried to contact the appraiser, but the man vanished. Next, his parents accused him, laying the blame at his feet without hardly speaking to him. And the evidence is incriminating." His well-cut suit lifted a bit at the shoulders. "So, we're here to find out who's taking advantage of Mr. Fitch. And why."

This time when Mr. Yost stood, he did it in a way that seemed to communicate that their conversation was over. The turn of his head and decisiveness of his movements stated that additional questions were not welcome. With just as many unresolved mysteries as before, Megan stood and thanked Mr. Yost. She shook his hand and took her sleepy canine with her out into the hall.

It was lunchtime, and varying fragrances filled the air from popcorn and coffee to soup and pizza. Mixed together, it wasn't what she'd consider pleasant. At the exit, she spotted Derek just outside, trying to maneuver three tall Styrofoam cups so he could reach for the door. She pulled it open for him and smiled.

"Thank you." His wide smile was handsome. "It was nice meeting you, Megan."

"You too," Megan said. Just as he walked past, Fred jumped up with a small yelp, nearly knocking all the drinks from his hands. "Fred!" Megan pulled him back, catching the look Derek gave the huge canine.

"I don't think he likes me." Derek laughed but didn't stop. "Have a good one," he called to her just before disappearing down the hall.

Megan turned to Fred with a scowl. "Why are you tormenting Derek?" She began walking to the car, wishing she could have been there to see what happened in the office while she was talking to Santiago. "He's so nice, and here you are picking on him."

Fred opened his mouth and let his tongue loll out.

Megan sighed, opening the back hatch to her little red car. Again, Fred turned his nose up, refusing to get in the back. "Particular, aren't you?" She closed it again and walked to the side door, eyeing Fred. The second she opened it, he hopped in with his tail wagging.

After stopping at a sub shop and ordering a turkey and veggie sandwich, toasted hot with honey mustard dressing, she returned to a park she'd noticed that morning. It was small and the play equipment rusty, but at least there was a table. She sat down and let Fred wander while she ate. Santiago's words were in her head, but they were jumbled. If he was really trying to communicate with her, what was it he wanted her to trace? Did he mean trace a person, as in follow them?

And who? Or maybe there was a document she needed to copy. She swallowed a big bite of turkey and melted cheese and flattened out the wrapper. Pulling a pen from her bag, she knew she had to get his words down before they were lost from her memory.

In the beginning, he'd sounded normal, talking to her about Seacrest and their friendship. She jotted as much down as she could remember. Then toward the end of their visit, he had specifically asked to speak to her for a little while. That was when things got weird. She started writing, closing her eyes between sentences to fully relive the conversation.

Please don't be... wait, no. *Please don't always be careful...* why would he phrase it like that? Then there was the part about danger and following her example. She scribbled out what she'd written and tried again. Why didn't she pay closer attention? It was just so unexpected, and she'd been so confused. She wrote out another sentence, squinting as she repeated it in her head. Was that what he'd said? She couldn't be sure.

Fred barked, having cornered a squirrel in a young pine tree. His big front paws were balanced on the trunk of the tree as it chattered angrily. His tail whipped back and forth. Megan turned back to her wrapper.

The world behind me. Edgewater Estates. No, he hadn't said Estates. But what was the last part? All she could remember was that he'd leaned forward to say goodbye and had said *trace* instead. She scribbled out another line and crumpled up the entire wrapper, tossing it in the trash. It was useless. Maybe if she could just figure out why he told her to trace something, that would give her a direction.

She glanced back at Fred to see he'd tired of barking but wasn't ready to give up. He'd lain down at the base of the tree, guarding his captive. But it was nearly 3 p.m., and they needed to be heading back to Seacrest. "C'mon, boy," she called, walking back to her car. But when she opened the door and looked back at him, he hadn't budged. "You want a treat?" she asked.

His head swiveled around and bolted from the tree, racing back to the car. Megan laughed and let him in. "Okay, one last stop, and *then* we're going home."

A small novelty store was right across the street from the gas station, so after filling up, Megan pulled into a parking space. It was oddly satisfying to park such a tiny car. She could practically park sideways and still be inside the lines. With Fred's leash in hand, she admired the quaint little shop with its forest green shutters and aged brick walls. An old red door creaked as it opened.

She'd hardly taken one step inside when a voice called out from somewhere behind the sloth toys in tiny Seattle t-shirts.

"No dogs allowed. Sorry."

Megan apologized and quickly and spun around, nearly colliding with the tall man behind her. "Oh, I'm sorry—" She froze at the sight of her ex-boyfriend. Of all people. He stood gawking back at her. Sandy brown hair under a Nike cap, freckles, polo shirt, and a golfer's tan. His light brown eyes flickered down to Fred and then back across her face.

"Megan," he said quietly.

They were locked in a strange sort of standoff, with Megan trapped between the unwelcoming shop and the one person in all Seattle who she'd been hoping to avoid.

"What are you doing here?" he asked, a smile settling on his lips.

"I could ask you the same thing," she said.

He responded by tipping his head toward the shop. "Authentic chocolate-covered macadamia nuts," he said with a wink. "They're the only place that carries the right kind. If you need to run in and get something, I'd be happy to stay here with your... dog."

The hesitation in his voice was perfectly normal, considering he was the only person besides her parents who knew how deep her fear of dogs was for most of her life. She looked down at Fred, considering. "Actually, I was just going to try to find him some dog treats, but they might not even have any."

"I'll go look." Jarron hurried back inside before she had a chance to object. Megan glanced in through the storefront window, watching as he pulled a box of macadamia nuts from a rotating rack. His height made his head visible even behind the rows as he wandered for a few minutes.

Megan glanced down at Fred. "I hope you're happy."

He wagged his tail.

When Jarron returned, he handed her a paper bag. "Something for you both."

He was standing very close, as he always seemed to do when he wanted to see her uncomfortable. But she was done allowing it. She squeezed around him, hoping for Fred to growl maybe a little, but he just sniffed at Jarron's feet.

"I was just visiting my parents for the day," she said. "I'm on my way home now." She peered into the bag to see huckleberry dog treats and a bag of dark chocolate peanut butter cups. He was always good at remembering her favorite things. When she looked back at him, his lips were twisted into a grin.

"Oh really?" he asked. "Visiting your parents?" He walked with her as she made her way back to her car. "Just stopping by the house to say hello?"

"Something like that," she said, wishing she were on the road already. Besides, something told her she didn't want him to keep talking. It was clear he could see right through her lies.

When they made it to the car, he leaned against faded red frame, gazing back at her. "Come on, Meg. Why don't you tell me why you're really here?"

"I told you." She cursed the hesitation in her voice but tried to keep her expression strong.

Jarron shook his head. "No, you didn't. You told me you came to Seattle to visit your parents, but your parents are out of town." He lifted his eyebrows, watching her as this information sank in. "They took a trip to Hawaii last week and asked me to watch their place for them."

Her stomach swirled with two levels of guilt. One for lying and one for being a horrible daughter who didn't even know her own parents were on a trip to Hawaii. She felt her cheeks flush.

"Look, I'm not trying to make you feel bad." His hand came to her shoulder. She took a quick step back, and he let it drop.

"Why are you still talking to my parents?" Her voice had hardened with anger and embarrassment. "I know you're just trying to get to me, but it won't work. I'm not coming back to Seattle."

"Everything was fine until I asked you to marry me," he said softly.

Megan looked up, meeting his eyes. He had a way of saying the perfect things, twisting what actually happened with how he wanted everyone to believe it happened. And he was good at it.

"I guess I'm just hoping we can take a step back and try again. If you don't want to get married, we don't have to." He took a small step closer but didn't reach for her again.

He's playing you. He's playing you.

She took her time in answering, first letting herself remember what it had really been like before he'd asked for her hand. The way he'd made decisions for her, combining their bank accounts, she suspected so he could control her finances. Always planning their evenings and vacations with the people he wanted them to be seen with and brushing aside her oldest friend. Allie hadn't liked Jarron; she'd seen through him almost the moment they'd met.

"Things weren't fine," she finally said, her voice quiet but firm. "You weren't good for me, Jarron. I'm sorry I didn't see it sooner."

"How can I change, then?" he asked, his eyes imploring. "How can I be good for you?"

He moved toward her, and she held a hand up, stopping him. "You can let me go."

Fred scratched at the door, and they both glanced at him. He lifted one foot and scratched again. Jarron leaned against the car door, and Fred's ears perked up as he watched him.

"You came to Seattle in this little clunker car, and now you're running back." He eyed her. "That tells me you're in trouble. Do you need anything? Money?" He pulled a wallet from his back pocket.

"No, Jarron, I don't need money, I'm not in trouble, and to tell you the truth, I love this car." She laughed at the look of disbelief he gave her. "A friend of mine is in a bit of trouble, yes. But there's nothing I can do for him, so I'm headed back."

"A friend, huh?"

She suddenly wished she'd kept her mouth shut. Jarron's eyes were practically glowing with intrigue, and with his professional connections as a semipro golfer, he just might be able to figure out who she came to visit. He crossed his arms in front of his chest as he stared back at her.

Fred barked, making them both jump.

"Whoa." Jarron took a step back.

"Fred, shhh," Megan said, although not very forcefully as she was grateful for the interruption. "We need to get going." She pulled the door open now that Jarron had backed away. "Thanks for helping my parents out."

Fred jumped into the seat with a haughty sniff.

"Bye, Megan."

She tried not to look at him as she got in the driver's side and backed out. Tried not to remember how gentle he could be sometimes, and how she used to love the way he said her name. One word from her and he would give her a place to live, find her a job, fill up her bank account. But she refused to give her life away so easily. As she watched him fade away in the rearview mirror, she felt a rush of relief at the freedom. It was worth more to her than the confining security of a relationship, like the one they'd had. And now she knew what she was going to do with it.

"Fred." She glanced over at her companion, who was snoring loudly. "We're going to get Santiago out of there."

Chapter Five

"No!"

Fred sprang out of the hole he'd been digging, completely covered in dirt. Megan groaned and went to survey the damage. It was right along the foundation, as always, and this time he'd dug a hole twice the size of any she'd seen him make before.

"Well." She sighed. "I guess I should be glad you're not unearthing someone else's foundation. Just mine."

Fred shook and sprayed dirt in all directions. She could feel the flecks hitting her in the head as she ducked, trying to avoid the onslaught. At least she was in her running clothes and already covered with sweat. She shook her ponytail out and decided to ignore the problem for a little while, at least until she could get warm. The Washington fog and chill had sunk to her bones, and she wouldn't be able to concentrate until she'd steamed it away with a hot shower.

She eyed her unapologetic dog as she passed. "I'll deal with you in a minute, mister." Her teeth chattered a bit, and Fred ignored her while he chewed on his foot, sitting on a hill of freshly excavated dirt.

That afternoon, after a shower for her and an easily forgotten scolding for him, they were back at the boardwalk with Fred firmly attached to a leash. The food truck festival phenomenon looked to be growing in popularity. Vendors nearly filled the parking lot, creating a bit of a hazard as hastily parked cars lined the roads. Megan managed to squeeze her little red car into a space between a van and a motorcycle and went to explore.

There were elephant ear scones and freshly made corn dogs, mile-high ice cream cones and the ever-popular coffee truck. It still had the longest line of them all. Megan looked over at the tea truck to see the top of Desmond's head as he reclined on his stool. There were no patrons. A stirring of sadness twisted in her chest as she thought of Margaret, and she wished there was something she could do.

Her eyes caught a glimpse of a poster plastered on the front of the ice cream truck.

EXCLUSIVE BLACK TIE FUNDRAISING EVENT

She moved closer, weaving through the crowd. There was a poster on the Mexican food truck as well and the Mongolian noodle truck. They all said the same thing. In three days, on Friday, they would hold a black-tie fundraising event for the Seacrest boardwalk. Tickets required, formal dress, and there was a list of attendees for everyone to drool over. But the price was a ridiculous two hundred dollars per person. Her heart sank a little as she told herself what a frivolous waste it would be for her to spend such an amount on one night.

She paused when she read the name Kenneth Blackburn on the poster. She hadn't spoken to him in weeks, but he was still a warm, buttery memory every time she thought of him. Their friendship had grown so seamlessly into something more. And yet, they'd only kissed minutes before he flew back to California, and their communication since then had been sparse at best.

Sure, she'd missed a call here and there and had felt too awkward to call him back, but she didn't want him to feel obligated to her. After all, he was an amazingly successful billionaire and was only in Seacrest to oversee the new housing development, Edgewater Estates.

Glancing up the hill to the cluster of new homes, Megan smiled, remembering a few pleasant experiences there... along with some not so pleasant ones.

"Pretty exciting, huh?"

Megan swiveled around to see Margaret standing next to her, gazing at the poster.

"A classy gesture to extend tickets to all the owners on the boardwalk too." Margaret's smile was practically ear to ear. "Here." She handed Megan an envelope.

"I noticed you hadn't been down to the shop in a few days, and I didn't want yours to get stolen or blow away in the wind. I'm sure I don't have anything nearly nice enough to call black tie, but what I have will have to do." She glanced back toward the tea truck where there was a single customer waiting. "Gotta go." She rushed away with a quick wave. "See you Friday!"

Megan stood in awe, looking down at the envelope in her hand. Slowly it dawned on her that she was going to the fundraising event... and Kenneth would be there too. She stared straight ahead, wide-eyed and heart racing.

Fred licked her hand, and she gasped, turning as he tugged his way toward the beach. She scanned the poster once more and tucked the envelope in her jeans pocket. Her thoughts wandered to a black dress in her closet she hadn't had the chance to wear yet. It would be perfect.

As she reached the sand, she slipped off her sandals and

followed Fred out to the edge of the surf. The waves along this part of the shore were friendlies, as she liked to call them. The beach sloped into the ocean so gently it left the water shallow for a hundred yards, making the waves tumble at an easy pace. It was the kind of beach parents of young children could relax at, and visitors with small dogs could enjoy.

Fred seemed to appreciate the easy water as well. He stomped through the wake as it fanned out along the beach and sniffed at the sand after it left, only to race away when it returned. Megan had dropped the leash and only watched him, letting the moment ease her mind. She knew there were more important things she should be worrying about than going to a party. Like Santiago's message to her. It was becoming more and more hazy with every minute that passed, which was frustrating. It had only been a few days since they returned home, and she'd never been able to completely write it down. It was so abstract that her mind just couldn't piece the words together exactly as he'd said them. She wasn't even sure she'd heard him correctly.

She took in a breath of salty air and sat in the warm, dry sand, watching the seagulls float along the surf, searching for sand crabs. Every few minutes one would dive and spear the water with its beak, chomping up a critter as it flew away. There seemed to be more crabs than she remembered, creating a formidable number of seagulls.

The flock of birds had beachgoers running away and diving under umbrellas as they circled the shore and back again. A cluster of rocks and tide pools at the far end of the beach looked like their favorite spot. A few dozen seagulls were perched atop a large boulder next to it, eyeing the unsuspecting marine creatures trapped within the pools.

Fred's loud panting pulled her from her musings, and she turned to see him soaking wet and dragging a long strand of seaweed toward her. Tan bulbs and large green leaves hung down from the vine as he hauled it ever closer.

"It's not coming with us," she warned, pointing a finger at him as he plodded up to her, soggy with saltwater. "No, Fred. You can't keep the seaweed. Drop it."

He sat, holding it in his mouth proudly.

The ride home was a stinky one, as the bundle of seaweed in the back of the car began to dry out. She hadn't noticed the smell nearly as much at the beach, but in her car, it was horrendous. Fred had quickly fallen asleep, mixing wet dog with the aroma of seaweed. Megan giggled as she looked over at him, shaking her head. He was a big kid, that was for sure. And if he was a big kid, that meant she was probably spoiling him rotten.

"And you know what?" She reached her hand over and pet his damp fur. "I'm fine with that."

It was Friday, 6:45 p.m., fifteen minutes before the black-tie fundraising event was scheduled to start... and suddenly Megan was questioning all her decisions in life. Looking into the mirror, her face was terribly flushed. The thin straps of her dress and slightly plunging neckline seemed only to accentuate the redness scattered across her neck like hives. It was the nerves that did it. But she'd had enough experience with it to know the color would fade in time.

She smoothed the fabric at her waist and spun slowly, admiring the shimmering black. It was beautiful. She'd bought it for a dinner she and Jarron were supposed to attend but never did. He'd made the mistake of asking her to marry him before then. Now, here she was in the little town of Seacrest, about to make an appearance at a formal event in the middle of a dozen food trucks.

Her heart raced as she looked back at herself in the mirror, eyes widened and scared. She couldn't go there alone, not when she was expecting to see Kenneth. What if he had a date? They'd never really spoken about being in an actual relationship, after all. There was probably nothing to his kiss. Maybe he kissed girls all the time for no reason.

She hurried to her phone and called the only person she could think of to turn to. "Crystal?" she said, her voice weak. "Are you going to the fundraising event tonight?"

"Well..." Crystal Chambers sighed. "Believe it or not, I'm dressed but haven't gotten off the couch in about an hour. I don't know why I was thinking of going. I'm sure it won't even—"

"Go with me!" Megan blurted out. "We can go together. That way if we leave early, it'll just look like we have something else to do."

"I guess..." She sounded like she'd already talked herself out of going.

"Please?" Megan begged. "I'm dressed too, and I really *really* don't want to go alone."

"Well, it *is* the first time I've worn heels in at least a year," Crystal said. Her breath gusted into the phone. "Okay, fine. Let's do it."

"Great!" Megan slid her feet into her black heels and bent down to buckle the straps. "I can be there in a few minutes."

"See you then." Crystal's voice sounded cheerful enough, leaving Megan free to be exhilarated again. Her heels clicked as she hurried to the front door. But when she opened it, a manilla envelop fluttered inside. She stepped back, looking down at it laying atop her toes. Then she remembered, she hadn't come in through the front door, not now that she had a car. The envelope must have arrived earlier in the day, and she was only just now seeing it. Fred lunged for it with his teeth, but she snatched it from the floor, intending to toss it onto the counter and get on with her night. "Fred, what's your issue with—"

She caught sight of the name Yost on the return label and paused. Closing the door slowly, she slid her finger under the seal and opened it. Inside, two pieces of paper were tucked neatly between the bubble wrap. Fred trotted over from his spot by the fire to whip her legs with his tail.

"Okay, Fred, hold on." Megan tipped the envelope, and the papers slid onto the counter. The first was a letter addressed to her. It was only a few sentences, and she scanned it quickly.

MS. HENNY, IT WAS A PLEASURE MEETING WITH YOU. I HOPE your trip home was in safety. I've sent you a transcript of your visit with my client, as requested by him.
    —Clive Yost, Attorney-at-law

SUDDENLY ANXIOUS, SHE FLIPPED TO THE NEXT PAGE, reading the words she'd been working so hard to remember. Their goodbye wasn't transcribed, but everything else was there. She read the beginning, when he'd seemed to be confessing his feelings for her. Then there was the strange ending. Reading it over again, it still made no sense. But what was the catch? What was she missing? She turned the page upside down and squinted, trying to trace the outline into something significant, but it was just a block with a jagged edge on one side. So, unless he was trying to tell her that Nebraska was the clue, she wasn't going about things the right way.

She sighed and set the page down, tapping her glossy red fingernails atop. Maybe he meant trace as in small. A tiny indication of something. But what? Her fingers continued tapping, and she stared off into the distance as she thought.

When Fred scratched at the door, she gasped and looked at the clock. 7:30? She hurried to open the front door. "Sorry, boy, you'll have to be quick!" He dashed outside, and she clicked through the house in her heels, rushing to her bathroom mirror. Checking her makeup, she added a smooth trail of lip liner and a swipe of gloss over her lips. She sprayed her hair, running her hands over the flyaways and tousling the wavy strands with a shake of her head.

It would have to do.

When she turned to leave, she caught sight of the South Sea pearl necklace on her countertop. She walked to it slowly, her heels clicking on the wood floor. Lifting it from the granite, she laid it against her skin, admiring the effect. It was a glorious accessory to her dress. She opened the clasp and secured it around her neck. Touching the pearls lightly, she gazed back at how her green eyes glimmered when contrasted with the black gems.

She rushed back to the door that was still open a few inches and looked out at the forest. Nightfall was still an hour away, but under the thick pine branches, the darkness had already come. She called for Fred and waited impatiently with one of her heels bouncing under her, clicking a tense beat. When he didn't appear, she closed and locked the door. It wasn't uncommon for him to spend several hours exploring the forest, after all. Maybe he'd been cooped up too much lately. She wasn't planning on staying more than a couple hours at the boardwalk, which meant she'd be home before it got too late, and Fred might miss her.

As she drove off, she decided to pick up a bed for the Great Dane as soon as possible. Something she could put outside on the deck so he could feel at home even when she was gone. She checked the rearview mirror one last time before her house was blocked by a wall of redwoods. Wherever he was, Fred was sure to be just fine.

When she arrived at Crystal's house, she couldn't help admiring the tasteful style. Everything looked new, even the landscaping. The edges and corners of each shrub and bush were trimmed and rounded to perfection. Her house was a clean, white ranch style, with everything on one level and windows surrounding the place. From the front door, she could see a beautiful expanse of wild grass and short ferns that looked out on a view of the ocean.

She stood in the entryway as Crystal hurried past in bare feet with her shoes in one hand. She held a finger up. "Just one minute!"

Megan admired her subtle blue dress, and the way the color glowed against her pale skin and blonde hair. The skirt was flowy and circular, whirling around her slender legs anytime she moved. She appeared again with one delicate blue gem-covered stiletto on one foot, and the other gripped between her teeth as she worked to clasp a diamond bracelet around her wrist.

"Here, let me help." Megan reached for the shoe and then paused. "Would you rather have help with the bracelet or the shoe?"

Crystal craned her neck, jutting her head forward with a toothy smile. Megan took the shoe from her mouth and knelt down, fitting it around her foot and starting on the clasp. "Thank you," Crystal said, dropping her arms to her side, one now glimmering in diamonds. "I really hadn't completely made up my mind until a few minutes ago. I just..." She shrugged. "I don't know, I guess I have sort of an awkward history with a few of the guests, that's all."

"Oh." Megan stood, intrigued. "Which guests?"

Crystal's blue eyes were more stormy than usual as her gaze skittered about the room. "Not really one person, per se.

I just used to be in the crowd that hosted fundraisers like this, instead of simply attending, if you know what I mean." She winked. "It's a drama-filled gossip fest every second of the day. I just needed to get out." She shrugged. "So, I did."

"I'm sorry." Megan's curiosity was ablaze, but she tried to respect her new friend's privacy, glad at least that she'd agreed to accompany her. "I didn't realize there was a history here. But I'm really glad you're going with me." She gave Crystal a quick hug and her friend seemed happy to drop the conversation.

She smiled back at Megan. "I'm excited too, thank you for forcing me to go."

They laughed as they made their way to Megan's car, and Megan hoped for both of them that the night would go well. She couldn't imagine any of the high-profile guests would be eager to start a scene, so she tried to settle down and enjoy the fun of attending a black-tie party. But when they pulled up to the boardwalk, she couldn't stop the excitement from fluttering away in her stomach.

Strings of lights were draped across the outdoor event space and sparkled beautifully. The ground had been layered in a maroon velvet material and planters with live palm trees and ferns were crowded with orchids and dahlias. A stage was constructed near the beach, and multi-colored lights strobed into the sky. The sun was just beginning to set, and the effect against the water was incredible.

Megan stepped out in awe at the elaborate setup, and on the other side of the car, Crystal did the same. When a man started walking toward her car, Megan could hardly stop her hands from shaking. With the sun behind him, she couldn't tell for sure who it was, but it looked a lot like Kenneth. He wore a tux and had an impressive build; one she thought sure she knew. One she remembered being held by. She walked to the front of the car, trying to get a better look.

And then she realized he wasn't looking at her. He walked up to Crystal and held his hand out, taking hers gently. She could make out his face now. Kenneth Bradburn. The man she couldn't wait to see again. His dark brown eyes and the Magnum PI mustache she'd giggled over. The man she'd kissed three weeks earlier.

He now gazed into Crystals' eyes, a woman she guessed he had a history with. Megan didn't dare look away from his face, even to see what Crystal's reaction might be. She was too busy sinking, her excitement slowly crushed as she studied his eyes. He was absorbed in Crystal's face, looking back at her with the expression Megan had wanted so desperately to see. Well, she was seeing it now... and it ached so bad it hurt. She felt suddenly sick and covered her mouth with one freshly manicured hand.

And then he turned to her.

His eyes widened, and she heard him gasp. But it didn't matter what he said to her after what she'd just seen. He'd spoken pretty loudly with just that one look. And Megan wanted nothing more than to disappear.

She ducked back into the car and started it quickly, ready to leave everyone at Seacrest behind.

Chapter Six

"Wait, Megan!" Kenneth dashed around the car, standing in front of it with his hands on the hood.

Megan could feel the tears coming, and she forced them back, taking a heavy breath. "Move!" she shouted, although her voice shook so badly, she could have been crying.

"Hold on." He held one hand up, staying in front of the car. Megan ground her teeth together, wishing he'd just get out of the way. Then again, a small part of her wanted to step on the gas. She put the car in park and crossed her arms in front of her, silencing her demons. She wouldn't run him over just yet.

The fact that she was completely overreacting crept into her mind slowly, making her face hot. She was sure her cheeks were blazing by the time he finally walked to her window and tapped on it. Now that she was feeling a little bit more rational, she wanted to disappear. She might as well have written her feelings on her forehead with the way she'd handled seeing them together. Who was she to jump to conclusions? She hardly knew either of them. Just because she'd spontaneously kissed Kenneth goodbye didn't exempt him from having a past, or even a future, with another woman.

Megan groaned lightly, mortified. Why hadn't she thought things through before trying to race away from what she'd felt was the ultimate betrayal? It had never been clearer to her how damaged her heart still was, and how much more time she needed to heal.

She brushed her hair from her face and took a steadying breath, feeling the shaking in her hands subside. When she rolled down the window, she kept her gaze on the steering wheel. But from the corner of her eye, she could see Kenneth lower down next to her. She couldn't bear the thought of what he might say, or what he would ask.

"I'm sorry, I just... don't want you to read into this," she said quietly, hoping Crystal couldn't hear. Carefully, terrified, she lifted her gaze to his eyes. They were just as she remembered, full of kindness. His mustache was lifted in a gentle smile, and he seemed completely unaffected by her strange behavior. "I didn't think you'd be here," he said quietly. "Margaret mentioned you were out of town."

"I was." Megan took another slow breath, feeling a tiny bit closer to normal after her sudden meltdown. She risked a glance at him again. "But I'm back now."

"Hmm." His smile widened. "I'm glad. If you want to leave, you're free to. I just didn't want you to think... uh," He hesitated.

"No, it's fine," Megan rushed, shutting off the car. She stepped out and Kenneth stood next to her, placing one hand at her back and gesturing toward the party with the other. "It's a beautiful night," he said. "Should we check things out?"

Crystal smiled back at them, standing elegant and confident. She didn't look upset or surprised and only gave Megan a small wink before she turned to the lights. The sun had sunk below the horizon, and the sky was lit up with color.

Crystal walked ahead of them, clearly giving them a moment together.

Megan's nerves would drown her if she didn't say something. She gripped Kenneth's jacket at both arms, stopping him. "I know we're not together," she rushed. "It's fine. I don't want a relationship right now, and this, what I..." She shook her head. "I was just really nervous about this party, I think. And I'm trying to get over some stuff—"

"Megan, it's okay," Kenneth said. He slid his hands down her arms, and she released her grip on his jacket. Holding her hands in his, he waited until she looked into his eyes. "I don't want you to feel committed to me when I'm not even here. That wouldn't be fair. And Crystal and I—"

"You don't have to explain," Megan interrupted. She meant to turn and follow Crystal, but Kenneth still held her hands. A grin twisted his mustache. "Crystal and I haven't seen each other in a long time." His voice was deep and calm. "We dated briefly, but more than that, I know how hard it must have been for her to make the decision to come tonight. She's had a difficult time with more than one of the donors here, but that's not for me to say."

Megan sighed, feeling suddenly exhausted. "She mentioned a little about it." She shook her head. "I had no idea—"

"Of course you didn't." Kenneth threaded her arm through his and began walking. "How could you? Besides, I have a very selective memory. I don't even recall the last few minutes."

"Oh, really?" Megan nudged him with her elbow, and he turned to wink at her.

"Really." His face softened, and his dark brown eyes glanced across her face. "You look beautiful, Megan."

"They have those homemade cinnamon roll bites," Crystal said, her voice raised over the noise of the crowd. She pointed to a line ahead of them. "Let's get some." She waited until they were instep beside her, and Megan was finally able to reset the evening.

With one quick breath, her mouth was watering at the cinnamon and sugar smell of warm, freshly baked goodness. She sighed with relief and stood in line next to Crystal.

"They say five new vendors arrived just last night," Kenneth said, their conversation becoming comfortably casual.

They talked about pastries and parties and the complexities of driving a food truck as they stood in line for cinnamon bites, and then Mongolian noodles, and finally a cup of tea. Kenneth's eyes found Megan often, and she allowed herself to revel in his attention, enjoying the side comments and silly jokes he seemed so full of. She laughed often and heartily, soothed by their company as the night wore on.

"If you would all gather near the stage," a voice boomed from three large speakers. "We'll start the bidding in thirty minutes."

"Already?" Kenneth said. He followed Megan and Crystal as they slowly wandered to the outer rim of the crowd. It was a large group for such a small town, easily two hundred people. Megan had met more than a few friends of Kenneth's by then, having chatted with CEOs and bodyguards alike. His life was certainly intriguing. When she glanced at a woman walking up to them, she assumed it was another acquaintance of Kenneth. She was a little younger than Megan, and her beauty was startling. Petite, yet elongated features and the skin of a rose petal. Her honey-brown hair was long and sleek, and her eyes were so dark they were nearly black. And they were trained on Megan.

"Hello," the woman said, glancing at the stage. "My name is Sylvia."

Her voice had a slight ending accent, the tail of each word

curving exotically. Megan smiled, glancing at Crystal and Kenneth to see them chatting casually and not paying any attention to this new person. "I'm Megan," she said, turning back to Sylvia. "Have we met before, or..." She let the question trail off, worried this person might be someone everyone knew by sight. Scanning the crowd quickly, she didn't see anyone taking notice.

"I'm sorry to just barge in on your evening like this," Sylvia said. She had a silk shawl that hung elegantly behind her back and around her arms, and she pulled it tighter. "I visited your rental shop before it closed. I'm sure you don't remember." She smiled shyly. "But I was so impressed by you and your courage to start a business on your own. I hope you stay. Seacrest is a town I've loved visiting since I was a child. We came as a family every year."

"So did I!" Megan said too loudly. She saw the slight look of surprise on Sylvia's face, although she wiped it away quickly. "Came here with my family, I mean." Megan couldn't help feeling thrilled at the small connection.

"What a small world," Sylvia said, her eyes flickering down at Megan's neck. "And might I add, what an incredible neck-lace. May I?" She reached her hand cautiously toward it.

"Yes, of course," Megan said. She took a small step closer, and Sylvia lifted the necklace gently, smoothing her finger across the beads.

"It's incredible," she repeated. "South Sea pearls, correct?"

"Yes, that's right," Megan said, surprised at her new friend's knowledge. No one that night had mentioned the necklace, not even Kenneth. "I almost didn't wear them. I'm not used to jewelry quite this nice."

"Oh, I'm glad you did," Sylvia crooned, her voice lost in contemplation as she admired the gems one by one. "Stunning."

"What's this?" Kenneth's voice could have been a gunshot

with the way Sylvia flinched back. In that fraction of time, Sylvia's eyes darted from Kenneth to half a dozen others before she settled again on Megan.

"It was so nice to meet you," Sylvia said, reaching her hand out and shaking Megan's. "I hope we see each other at Seacrest again sometime."

"Yes, me too." Megan squeezed her hand warmly. She couldn't wait to see Sylvia again. Her voice had been a joy, the way it rang with distinct tilts and curves. She glanced back in the direction her new friend had gone, but she was too late. Sylvia had vanished in the crowd.

"Someone you know?" Crystal asked.

Megan shook her head, "We just met. She came to my shop when it first opened, I guess."

"That's nice." Crystal's attention turned to the front as the auction began, as did Kenneth's and Megan's. There was a three-night stay at the newly remodeled bed-and-breakfast by the lighthouse being auctioned first. Megan considered placing a bid. She'd never been to the lighthouse, as it was an hour trip down the coastline, but in only two minutes it had already gone well past $500. She let the bidders with deeper pockets than hers battle it out. And battle, they did, up until the winner placed a $1200 bid. She peered through the crowd, trying to make out who'd won, but it was to no avail.

Next was a large basket of items and gift cards donated from shops on the boardwalk. It made Megan feel a little guilty for not contributing, but she had no choice. Her shop was taking a break until she could figure out what to do with it. A car was auctioned off from the little car lot she'd visited, and there was a long lineup of items still to go. Vacation packages, deep-sea fishing excursions, and bundles of mouth-watering goodies and charming housewares. It would easily take up another hour. And with the sun long since set, the temperature dropped by the minute.

Megan wrapped her arms around herself, rubbing her sides. The black dress was beautiful, but not exactly functional. Something touched her shoulders, startling her. She looked back just as Kenneth draped his jacket around her. "Oh, thank you," she said, holding onto the fine, sleek material. It smelled good too, like rugged Pacific meets down-to-earth lumberjack. But Kenneth's eyes didn't linger, and his attention turned back to the auction. He seemed entirely caught up in it, but with her body no longer shivering, she was glad he'd somehow noticed her discomfort. Although if she were being honest with herself, she would have liked a little more of his attention.

She glanced at him again, quickly admiring his face before turning away. The auction was clearly out of her range, so she scanned the crowd instead. First looking for Sylvia, she quickly gave up and tried to find Margaret instead. A woman like her would be drinking up an evening like this one. As she searched, something caught her eye. She peered into the darkness behind the food trucks and string lights to see Fred standing there. Tall and alert, he appeared to be staring right back at her.

"Fred," she called, trying to keep her voice below the chatter of the crowd. His silhouette didn't move. Crystal turned around to look back at him. "Is that your dog?" she asked.

"Yeah." Megan smacked her hand against her thigh, although the suit coat muffled it. Fred's ears lifted, but he still didn't move. His head snapped back and forth as he looked around and then returned to staring back at her.

"I wonder what he's doing," Crystal mused. "Maybe he's scared of the big crowd."

Although Megan had never been in such a crowd with him before, she'd never sensed an apprehension from Fred about anything since he'd come to live with her. "I don't know."

She called him again, but he dashed away suddenly, disappearing behind the food trucks. "Hopefully he just wants to be curled up by the fire. It's a little later than I'd expected to be gone." She turned back to Kenneth to find he was watching them. But when their eyes met, he turned to the front and lifted his hand, placing a bid.

"Winner!" the announcer shouted. Megan stood on her toes, interested to see what he'd won. The announcer continued in a loud, fast-as-lightning voice, describing a beautiful home-spa pedicure set.

"Finally," Kenneth said, grinning. "I've always wanted one of those."

Megan and Crystal looked back at him silently for a moment before breaking into laughter.

"What?" Kenneth lifted his chin, as if protecting his pride. "Maybe I enjoy smooth feet."

"Mm-kay," Crystal said, patting him dramatically on the shoulder. "That sounds so like you."

"Well, you don't know me as well as you might think." Kenneth crossed his arms in front of him, looking a little irritated. "I'm going to go claim my prize." With that, he marched through the crowd.

"Uh..." Crystal was wide-eyed, watching him leave. "Do you think he's upset for real?"

"I don't think so," Megan said. "But either way, he has to come back eventually to get his jacket." She grinned, and Crystal laughed.

Meanwhile, the auction moved to the next gift basket. A blanket and candles with two well-aged bottles of wine.

"I heard you went to see Santiago," Crystal's voice was lowered, and she eased in closer to Megan as she spoke. "Is he really in jail?"

Megan hesitated, but then she nodded, keeping her voice as quiet as possible amidst all the commotion. "He is. I went to visit him, but the things he said were so confusing. He wasn't even making sense."

"Hm." Crystal squinted as she thought. "Well, that doesn't sound like him. He's pretty articulate for a younger man." She shrugged. "The only time I couldn't understand him was when he spoke his native language." She shook her finger at Megan. "And I know a little bit of Spanish, but I guess it's a slightly different dialect with him being from Spain."

Megan sighed. "Well, he was definitely speaking English." She suddenly noticed Crystal was holding herself tightly and beginning to shiver. "Oh my gosh, I'm so sorry." She took one arm out of Kenneth's coat and squeezed in next to Crystal, lifting the coat around her.

Crystal laughed, sliding her arm through the one sleeve. "Normally I'd object, but I'm freezing." She laughed, her voice jittery as she shivered at the same time.

"Yes, you are. Your hands are ice." Megan wrapped her arm around her friend and cringed a little as Crystal's cold hand wrapped around her as well. Now that they each had an arm slid through either side of Kenneth's coat, they looked like a strange sort of monster, short and boxy and with two shades of hair. They giggled back and forth as they both leaned and tugged against the other.

"Maybe I should have rented two coats," Kenneth said. Megan swung around, bringing Crystal with her, and looked back to see Kenneth holding a huge basket filled with spa items and tied in elaborate pink chiffon. His irritation seemed to have melted away, and he laughed in small bursts, as if he were trying to hold it back but couldn't. "You two look..." He shook his head, his eyes trailing from their tops to their toes. "Cold, actually. You still look cold."

"Hey, when they say black tie, they should say black tie

and bring a parka." Megan laughed at herself, but she couldn't help glancing back at where Fred had been. Plus, thoughts of Santiago were digging at her subconscious. "I think, uh—" Megan glanced at Crystal with a question in her eyes. "I think we're ready to leave?"

"Yeah," Crystal agreed, still squeezing Megan tight with one arm under the coat. "I think that's a good call." It had warmed slightly between them, but there was still the fact that both of their dresses only extended to mid-thigh.

"Here, I'll walk you to your car." Kenneth usually would have placed one arm gently along her back, but as it was, he didn't seem to know what to do with the both of them. Plus, Megan was sure they were going to topple over with each step she took, but removing the coat was out of the question. She had begun to shiver with it on, even sandwiched next to Crystal.

They got to her car, and Crystal hopped in immediately. "Bye, Kenneth!" She pulled the blanket from the back seat and wrapped up as Megan turned to Kenneth.

One side of his coat was still threaded through her arm while the other hung down her back. He balanced the huge basket in one arm and reached forward to lift the coat back onto her shoulder.

"I can just get it from you tomorrow." He paused with his hand at her neck, holding the collar of his coat, looking into her eyes.

But in the next second, he pulled his gaze away. He walked to the back of her car and opened the hatchback, placing the basket in the trunk. "I think you ladies can make better use of this."

Megan stood right where he'd left her, watching him. But when he closed the hatch, she jumped and hurried to the driver's side. "Thank you," she said, stepping inside and twisting the key in the ignition. She turned in her seat, looking back at him. "But I think it would be more fun if you joined our spa night." Her heart was pounding as she tried to look calm, but he only tipped his head to the side.

"Not tonight, I'm afraid." He stepped onto the sidewalk. "I have an early meeting."

"Okay. Yeah, that's fine," she stuttered, feeling foolish. "Goodnight!" She leaned to the side and tried to get a look at his face, but the car was too small.

When she pulled away from the curb, there was a strange sort of awkwardness between them, although she wasn't quite sure why. She watched Kenneth in her rearview mirror as he shrank in the distance, gazing back. He shifted his weight and threaded one hand through his hair before sinking his hands into his pockets. Everything together had her realizing... there was something he wanted to say. But for some reason he hadn't said it, and she worried it was all because of her meltdown a few hours earlier.

But he hadn't turned it against her the way Jarron would have. He didn't twist her words until she was apologizing for everything she could think of. He'd only calmed her fears and told her he was happy to see her. It had her feeling warm and toasty, although it could have been the heater that was now blasting out ninety-degree air.

She glanced in her rearview mirror one last time, looking at the glow of the event through the trees and finding herself counting down until the next day, when she would see him again.

Chapter Seven

"You really didn't have to share with me, you know," Crystal said. But then she sighed and sank down in her chair with her feet submerged in bubbly, lavender infused saltwater.

Megan's feet were lost in bubbles as well. "I know," she mumbled through her relaxation. "But what fun would that be?"

It was nearly midnight, and they were in Megan's bathroom with identical tubs full of spa pedicure products. The heavenly scent filled the room. "I'm glad Fred came back to the house on his own. It was a little odd to have him follow me to the party and then refuse to come up to us. It wasn't like him." Megan said, her thoughts wandering.

"Also, when did you date Kenneth?" She glanced at Crystal to see her friend's eyes pop open.

"Uh, that's an abrupt subject change." Crystal laughed and then yawned. "But I'm glad you asked. I meant to talk to you about it all night." She sat up in her chair, leaning over her knees. She was wrapped in a robe and her blond curls had flattened into sleepy waves. "We respect each other, and he knows how hard it was for me to be there tonight, but that's all it was."

Her eyes flickered to Megan and back to her toes. "I know it probably looked like more. He's a very compassionate person."

"And the time you dated?" Megan swished her toes in their lavender bath, feeling nosy but also refusing to let it go.

Crystal stared at her feet for what felt like a long time. Finally, she nodded. "Yeah, we dated." Her head tilted to the side. "Almost eight years ago now. It was actually before I'd come to Seacrest. We met at a Christmas party and had a lot of fun together. He was always playing these harmless pranks, but in our crowd, nothing is harmless. People take things deadly serious." She shrugged and smiled back at Megan. "I thought it was hilarious, actually."

They both laughed, but Megan couldn't help glancing at her, waiting for more.

"One time—" Crystal had to choke back her laughter before she could continue. "He snuck a dye into the punch fountain that turned everyone's mouth bright blue. Try to have people take you seriously when they can't look away from your tongue when you talk." She sighed, wiping a laughter tear away. "That was the most interesting year's end report I think I ever sat through."

"So, what happened then?" Megan asked. So far, all she'd heard was that Kenneth was amazing. Why would they break up?

"Well…" Crystal shifted in her chair, no longer yawning. Her trip through memory lane seemed to have woken her, and now she looked a little uncomfortable. "It was mostly that I could tell he wasn't feeling it very deeply. I mean, he's a great guy, and we were both quite a bit younger, so it makes sense he wasn't looking for anything too serious." She glanced at Megan.

"I was traveling quite often at the time, and he was always happily surprised to see me when I was around. We'd go out and act like a couple." Her eyes found Megan again. "You know. But I quickly heard stories about the women he was with when I was gone, which was the majority of the time. People thought I was being a fool... not that I cared what they thought. But it does make you question things when you hear about a dozen women who've stood in your place, held his hand, and looked into his eyes. You start to wonder how much of it was real."

With a sigh, she lifted her feet from the water and wrapped them in a towel. "In the end, I knew I was just a fun idea every now and then, like he enjoyed the escape from his normal type of woman. But the moment I left, I was out of his head. And *forgettable* is not what I've ever wanted to be for anyone." Her lips were lifted in a gentle smile when she sat back in her chair and crossed her arms, clearly finished.

Megan was increasingly uncomfortable, having taken every word Crystal spoke and applied it to herself. Their stories were entirely too similar. She even met Kenneth over a prank, and he kissed her just before leaving town. And after that? She hadn't heard from him since. Now she was back at a party with him, and his attention was all hers. It didn't sit well.

"That was a long time ago," Crystal repeated, eyeing Megan seriously. "I can already tell that he's changed."

She was clearly trying to ease Megan's fears, but it only had her cheeks warming with embarrassment. Her and Kenneth hadn't gotten nearly as serious in their relationship —if you could call it that. Mostly, they'd had a moment together just before he left Seacrest. Did that really count as anything? Besides, she still needed time to be on her own and figure her life out. A relationship was the last thing she needed, even if it felt like what she wanted.

Megan lifted her feet out of the water that was now luke-warm. She wrapped them in a towel and tried to sort out a response.

"Have you heard back from Santiago?" Crystal asked.

Megan froze for a moment, swapping out thoughts of Kenneth for thoughts of Santiago. "Not a thing, actually. I think he's waiting for me to respond, but I'm not really sure what he told me in the first place. It's a little confusing."

"Well, maybe something will come to you tonight in your dreams—" A yawn cut off Crystal's response, and she held her hand up. "Sorry, I really should get home."

"Sure thing." Megan hopped up and went in the front room, eyeing Fred asleep by the fire. He'd miraculously left them alone the entire time they were soaking their feet. Megan thought for sure she'd be fighting him away from the sudsy fun the whole time. He must really be tired. He lifted one sleepy eyelid to glance at her. "Be good, Fred," she pointed at him. "I'll be right back."

He closed his eyes and sighed, making his lip flap in response.

"Good boy."

After dropping off Crystal, she drove home deep in thought. It was clear she needed to be careful when it came to Kenneth, but she also didn't want to use stories about his past against him. If he ever tried using her past against her, there was far too much to work with. She wanted them both to start with clean slates. But she also didn't want to be naive.

She pulled up to her house and smiled. It was beautiful at night with the windows glowing in the firelight. Stepping out of the car, she only walked a few steps before hearing a thud from inside. Her head perked up, and she rushed up the steps, hurrying to open the door. She swung it open and saw an empty rug where Fred had been sleeping before. Following the sounds of dog mischief brought her back into the master bathroom... where she'd forgotten to dump out the tubs.

He stood with his front paws in one tub and his back in the other, stomping and jumping and entirely unaware she was home. He paused for a moment with his tail wagging so hard, his body curved side to side.

"Ahem," she said loudly.

Jumping out of the tubs, he slipped and flopped on the ground. The soapy floor proved to be entirely too slippery as he slopped this way and that, trying to get to his feet again. Megan laughed, carefully making her way over to him and gripping his collar. She pulled him up from the floor, and then he shook.

"Fred!" She laughed as she shielded herself from the onslaught of sudsy water. Then she opened the cupboard where there were always six towels waiting for just such an occasion.

"Stay." She eyed him, and he opened his mouth so it looked like he was smiling back. Surely, he knew what he was doing. He was too smart for his own good. She began laying towels on the floor and then draped one across his back, rubbing him down. "At least you'll smell good, like lavender."

Eventually he was back in his place, curled up by the fire, and Megan filled a mug half full with hot cocoa. She sat down and reached for a blanket that was rolled up on one side of the couch. Snuggled up, she watched the fire and sipped the hot drink, allowing it to calm her. She needed to return to the transcript she'd been sent, and she needed to figure out just what she was going to do with her shop. But as her breath slowed and her eyelids became heavier, she decided she would get to those things tomorrow.

In her dream, Santiago was speaking too quickly. He wasn't making sense, and she was trying to ask him to slow down, but she couldn't get any words to come out of her mouth. Finally, she realized he was speaking Spanish. He paused and lifted his hand up, holding up three fingers.

"Tres," he said, staring into her eyes. "Tres."

Megan gasped awake and sat up suddenly. She was still on the couch, and her empty mug tumbled to the floor. "Three," she whispered. "He was saying three."

Bursting with energy, she hopped up from the couch and raced back to the counter to snatch up the paper, repeating the word *three* in her head. But three what? What did he mean by that? There might be an address at Edgewater with the number three, but why would he mumble all this incoherent stuff? It had to mean something. She scanned the words over and paused, shaking her head. She read them again. What was he saying? Maybe there were three words he wanted her to put together. Scanning the page again, she could make out a dozen different messages, but none of them told her what he wanted. The words blurred as she continued to stare.

"Ugh," she mumbled. "Fred, I still don't know what he wants me to do." She looked over to see Fred sleeping. "Maybe you're right. I should wait until morning." She yawned. "Maybe he'll come to me in another dream."

But no more dreams came that night, and she woke feeling cranky and unrested. She reached for the Red Bull in the back of her fridge and cracked it open, drinking half and putting it back on the shelf. Then she poured a bowl of cereal and sprinkled a handful of blueberries on top. Fred seemed content to sleep in, and she glanced over at him as she ate, a little envious. But her mind wouldn't let her sleep any longer. She had the sense that Santiago needed her, and she was determined to find some answers.

After she finished eating, she slipped out the door, needing a change of scenery while she thought. She drove to the boardwalk and unlocked her shop. The room smelled clean and new. With a sigh, she gathered the few pieces of junk mail that had been delivered and locked it up again. She passed Crystal's shop to see it wasn't opening until the afternoon. Margaret's books and tea shop was next door, and she wandered in to see Margaret looking a little frazzled. She was scribbling into a notebook, and her gray hair bounced impressively with each word she wrote.

"Hello, Margaret," Megan said with a smile. "Is everything all right?"

"Oh heaven's, no," Margaret grumped. "That boy is going to run me clean off the boardwalk. He seems to think the food truck I started is just for fun. But to pay for the loan, I need him to actually sell tea!"

"What do you think needs to change?" Megan asked. "Maybe I can help. I've got some time right now. Do you want me to go down there?"

"And do what?" Margaret looked defeated, her arms lifting and then falling against her sides. "People aren't coming in for tea."

"Well, what if you sold something in addition to the tea? Something none of the other trucks sell."

She thought back to her fundraising days in college. It was practically the only thing that kept her from starving to death. "Homemade donuts are always a hit, plus you can smell them for a mile at least." She laughed. "Hungry stomachs can't resist. And they go really well with tea."

She lifted an eyebrow, taking a break from scribbling on her paper. Megan glanced down at it to see an old-fashioned ledger, and the numbers were dwindling quickly. "I suppose it couldn't hurt." She took a deep breath. "I have a small kitchen in back. Do you think that would do?"

"Sure," Megan said. Her little college apartment had been big enough, and Margaret's would probably be twice the size. The thought of making a batch of donuts was freeing, allowing her mind to rest from the constant effort of solving puzzles. "Do you have ingredients here?"

"No." Margaret shook her head, looking glum again.

"Don't worry about it." Megan lifted her purse over her head. "I'll just run and get some and whip up a double batch. Let's just see how it goes today." She gave Margaret a quick squeeze, but her friend still looked doubtful.

Hurrying to the market, she bought a big bag of flour and other ingredients. There was a café in the front of the building, and she watched the customers as she stood in the checkout line. Each one of them had a pastry with their coffee, which was encouraging. Maybe Margaret didn't sell coffee, but Megan also knew for sure that the coffee hut didn't sell pastries. This just might give her the winning edge.

As she pushed her cart loaded with groceries, she noticed a man sitting at one of the small circular tables alone. He turned his head, and she couldn't believe it. She pushed her cart a little closer just to be sure. When she was right next to him, there could be no mistaking his handsome face. She tapped his shoulder. "Derek Montel?"

He turned to her and smiled, although it didn't reach his eyes. The sadness on his face was the noticeable kind. "Ms. Henny, I was hoping to run into you here. I Just came down for a little vacation, and it's everything you said and more. The best place to relax and enjoy the natural coastline that I've ever found. Thanks for that."

She scooted her cart a little closer and sat down. "So, you just had a bit of vacation time, then?"

He took a big gulp of his orange juice. "No, I was fired." There was an empty pastry wrapper on the table in front of him with some crumbs that looked suspiciously like they'd come from blackberry scones.

"Fired?" Megan couldn't imagine it. He was far too professional a person for something like that. She shook her head.

"Yeah, I was trying to research a lead on my own before divulging it to Yost. But he found out and tried to pin it on me. It was impulsive of him, but I guess he's been double-crossed by an associate before." He sighed, taking another swig of orange juice.

"What were you researching?" Megan crossed her arms atop the table, continuing in a whisper. "Did it have to do with Santiago?"

His eyes lifted to hers, and a small grin touched his lips. "I believe so."

"C'mon then, let's figure it out together." She grabbed his hand. "You can go back to Yost with the answers and get your job back. If you want it, that is."

He turned to her with something close to a smile. "Okay, let's see what you've got." He pushed his cup to the side. "We were being recorded in the office, as you know, and one day I noticed an icon on my phone that must have been added by someone else. I know I never downloaded it. A malware app. The scorpion recorded conversations at a close distance and sent them to the host person." He eyed Megan. "But I have no idea who this person was. They might have been working with clients of Santiago. As for me, I believe they're the same clients of his that were searching for a specific piece of jewelry. A Mr. Carter Dewald and his fiancée."

"The piece that Santiago could never find?" Megan asked. "Do you know what it was?"

"No." He ran one hand through his black hair. "I had a phone interview with Mr. Carter, but didn't get anything out of him. The only thing he told me was that he'd hired someone to locate the piece for him."

"Do they know you by sight?" Megan asked, conspiring.

Derek seemed a little suspicious of her question, and his head tilted. "Yes, in fact. We met at a conference last year. Carter, that is. I haven't met his fiancée. All I know about her is that she's French. Had a tough upbringing in an orphanage until she was adopted by a billionaire couple who couldn't have kids. She's a bit of a dreamer because of it."

"What is it that Carter Dewald does, exactly?" The wheels in Megan's head were turning.

"Investment banking," Derek was still eyeing her.

"So technically, I could hire him to beef up my retirement portfolio? Maybe ask him a few questions about his fiancée?"

"Absolutely not." Derek's smile disappeared. "That would be much too dangerous."

"You said his office is close to yours? I'm sure I could find it easily enough." Megan smiled, but Derek still looked like his answer was no. But it wasn't really up to him. Megan already knew she was going to drive down there. Why not? Mix up some donuts today, drive out to Seattle, and interrogate a banker tomorrow. She had time for both.

Derek held his hands up as if trying to stop her. "Now, hold on."

Megan gave him the look that meant she was serious. The one that never worked on Fred. But on Derek, it seemed to at least give him pause. After a moment, he took a deep breath.

"There are dangerous people intertwined in this, Ms. Henny," he whispered. "Whoever Mr. Carter hired to track this jewelry down is likely a very experienced criminal. I can't allow you to put yourself in harm's way."

"I think this will help me figure out what Santiago has been up to," Megan whispered back. "He tried to tell me something in some sort of code, and I honestly cannot figure it out. Maybe this will help."

Megan rested one hand on his arm. "Look, I'm going to do it whether you want me to or not. I need to help Santiago. He's important to me, and I believe he's completely innocent. But I really would love to work with you, instead of alone.

You know, get your advice on espionage and interrogation tactics and all that." She winked.

Derek's dark eyes studied hers, and then he stood from his chair. "C'mon, Ms. Henny, let's walk and talk." As he was pushing in his chair, he leaned in close to her ear. "First lesson, never stay in one place too long." Megan's heart skipped a beat as she realized what he was telling her with that one tip.

Her plan to interrogate a very powerful investment banker... was on.

Chapter Eight

✦✦✦

The donuts turned out just like Megan remembered. She could practically hear the collegiate band playing and the fans cheering. She loaded up a half dozen boxes and began transporting them to the tea truck. There was a new sign hanging on one side of the front counter in big, bold lettering.

HOT, HOMEMADE DONUTS.

It seemed to be working. For the first time, there was a small line of four people waiting. Megan helped Desmond with the transactions, pleased that every customer ordered at least one cup of tea as well.

As for Desmond, she tried to make conversation often, switching from cars to sports to music. He didn't seem particularly enthusiastic about any of them. As they got to the last box of donuts, she tried a new tactic.

"What did you do over the weekend?" she asked, expecting to hear about the black-tie event. It seemed every person in Seacrest had been there. But Desmond didn't comment on the auction or the music or the food trucks. He inclined his head toward the beach.

"I was out there for most of the weekend."

"Do you surf?" Megan handed a package of three donuts and a cup of steaming honey lavender tea to a customer. Behind her, Desmond laughed. It was the first time she'd heard him laugh before, and she turned around with a smile. Happiness looked good on him. His shaggy hair and amused expression gave him more of a cozy beach vibe instead of the indoor-all-the-time look he usually sported.

"Nah, this beach is too mellow for surfers. Just beginners go here. I was actually on the rocks." He glanced back at her, looking a little unsure. But after only a moment, he continued. "There's been a big spike in hermit crabs this season, and no one knows why. I heard it was a warm swell of water that brought a lot of them to our beach when they would usually settle farther south." He brushed his hair out of his face. "So, it's made the seagull population boom as well, and the city doesn't like that too much. Have you noticed?"

Megan looked out at the beach. Now that he mentioned it, there were more seagulls than she'd ever seen along the waves. They stood like little soldiers at attention, and then a dozen of them would race after a receding wave and pick at the sand.

"They're decimating the hermit crab population," Desmond sighed.

Megan was temporarily stunned at hearing him use the word *decimated*. She smiled as she listened to him explain about something for which he was truly passionate. Finally.

"I hate to see them destroyed like that. Hermit crabs are so cool. They're super friendly and fun and easy to take care of. But there are a lot of laws against taking them away from the beach, so I just find as many as I can and I carry them out on the rocks when the waves are out." He sighed, looking out at the food truck lot. There weren't many customers now that the lunch rush had ended. "It's not much. I wish I could do more, like scare the seagulls away."

"I wonder if there's something you could do," Megan said, seeping a bag of lemon zest in hot water. "Since it's so unusual, I mean. Maybe the city would work with you on a temporary basis."

"Like how?" Desmond's eyes were alight for the first time as he looked back at her.

"I know someone who has close ties with the mayor." Megan punched his arm playfully. "Let me see what I can do."

She stayed an hour longer and then let Desmond handle the last part of the day. Besides, Margaret always came to help with closing, and Megan didn't want to have to refuse another paycheck. Helping with the food truck wasn't about money. She just wanted to see it succeed.

Before heading home, she got a text from Derek asking her to call. She did so right away, sitting in the parking lot in her little red hatchback with the engine running.

"Hey," he said. His voice was so quiet, she turned down the radio before answering. "Hi Derek, how's it going?"

"Good. When's your appointment?"

"Monday," she said, feeling a little taken aback by the clear tension in his voice.

"Okay." He was quiet for a moment. "I can't go with you, but I'd like you to keep in touch with me. Can you do that? I'll just be a phone call away if you need anything."

"Sure,"

"And I'm sending over some questions for you to ask."

"Thanks, Derek." Megan pulled out of the parking lot and headed for home. "I'm sure it will be fine."

"What did Santiago say to you?" he asked. "The thing you couldn't figure out. What was it?"

"Oh." Megan reviewed the words in her head, trying to get them right. But the way they were mixed up uncertainly made it harder. After a moment, she shook her head. "It's so hard to remember them. I can give you a call when I get home and read it to you if you'd like."

"Yes, but I've got a flight in a few minutes." He sighed. "Job interview. Give me a call tomorrow first thing, okay?"

She agreed, and they ended the call, but she felt anxious at the idea of an interview with Carter Dewald all on her own. She'd rather gotten used to the idea of Derek going with her. Derek's text came through and she scanned it, finding everything was fairly straight forward. Ask about his fiancée, plans for a wedding. Make it sound like small talk.

When she made it back to her house, she walked to the porch overlooking the forest and settled down on the top step. Fred had been on his own most of the day, and she was expecting him to come bounding out of the trees any minute. She whistled for him and heard him bark from not too far away.

"Sounds like he's on his way."

With a gasp, she spun around to see Kenneth at the other end of her deck. He hesitated halfway up the steps. "Sorry," he said. "I tried to call but there was no answer."

Fred's energetic panting interrupted them as he appeared from the forest. He had something in his mouth, and he bounded over ferns and fallen trees. But when Kenneth joined Megan on the deck, Fred dug his feet in and skidded to a stop. Megan could now see there was an envelope in his mouth.

"Fred, what do you have there?" she asked, using a tone that she hoped would convey her displeasure with him. "Are you stealing mail?"

Kenneth sat down next to her on the step, and Fred huffed out a startled bark. The way he usually did when a stranger would walk by with their hoodie pulled down over their face.

"It's okay, Fred. C'mon," she encouraged. But Fred just dashed back into the trees.

"Ugh," Megan groaned. "Now I'll have to wait another two hours for him to come back." She smiled at Kenneth. "I really should make him act like a pet now that he is one, but I feel bad taking away his freedom."

Kenneth sat on the step next to her, looking out into the trees. "One way to look at it would be that it's for his own protection. He might meet a wild animal or a dognapper." He shrugged. "He really is a valuable dog."

"Hm." Megan didn't like the way her stomach turned at the thought of someone stealing Fred. "Yeah, you're right. Besides, he seems pretty happy to have a home."

"He is." Kenneth nodded. "I've never seen him happier than when he's with you. So, it's not really a punishment. How could it be?" A smile pulled his lips upward as he looked back at her. He stood abruptly and turned back toward his car. "I almost forgot. I came because I need to return my suit to the rental shop, but I have to have it dry-cleaned first. Do you have the coat?"

"Oh." Megan stood quickly. "Here, I'll grab it for you." She went inside, pausing at the doorway. "You're welcome to come in for a minute... if you want."

He shrugged, and it appeared her offer was only mildly interesting. "I could stay for a little while, I guess."

With a sinking feeling, Megan went to fetch the coat. Every once in a while there was a glimmer of something in Kenneth's eyes, but then it would vanish, and he'd look completely bored. She sighed, draping the coat over her arm. He was inside, leaning against the kitchen counter. She considered telling him about her plans for the next day. He was a businessman, after all. Maybe he'd have some advice on how to interrogate one.

In the end, she decided against it. He would probably

think she was crazy. But, there was a chance he might know something about Santiago. She handed him the coat.

"I've been trying to figure out what's going on with Santiago." She pulled out a barstool, hopping up on it. "I want to help him." When she looked into his eyes, he was nodding slowly. "Have you heard anything?"

He shifted his weight and adjusted the coat hanging across his arm. "I have, actually." He sighed. "The family has had their issues for a few years at least, what with Santiago refusing to attend Stanford, their alma matter. He wanted to experience real life, so he calls it."

"I didn't realize that." Megan shrugged. "But there's a lot about Santiago that is still mysterious to me. He doesn't like to talk about his past or upbringing."

"No." Kenneth smiled. "That's for sure."

"Why is that?" Megan could tell there was more Kenneth knew, but he shook his head.

"I really shouldn't say." He tucked the coat around his arm and turned to the door. "I've got to get this over to the cleaners. Can I give you a call later? I'm headed out of town tomorrow."

"Yeah, I'd like that." Megan wasn't sure why he was running away. Maybe he really did need to get to the cleaners fast, but he was Kenneth Bradburn for goodness' sake. Surely he had half a dozen assistants to do that. In the end, she waved goodbye to his back-and-forth, confusing personality and secretly hoped he would return soon. Her heart needed to heal, yes. But it also needed to be filled, and Kenneth always managed to make that happen.

Just as the sound of his car on the gravel drive faded, there was a scratch at the door. Megan smiled as she went to open it. There stood Fred, yet again, covered in dirt. When she didn't move out of the way or swing the door open for him, he plopped his hind end down on the deck and looked up at her, as if asking what her problem was.

Megan laughed. "You're just too much, aren't you, Mr. Astaire?" She lifted an eyebrow at him and pointed, touching his nose. "Stay."

He sneezed, spraying her hand in dirt and saliva.

"Ah, well played, Fred. I need to stop doing that." Holding her hand up, she hurried to the kitchen sink, washing it then soaking a towel next. She wiped Fred down and again walked him to the bathroom tub. It was beginning to be a tiring routine, and she lectured him on the proper way to stop a bad habit, telling him it would take time but she could help. And as he jumped out of the tub and shook, soaking her yet again, she was at least happy that it was with lavender-smelling doggy shampoo. It was the little things.

When she went back into the living room, Fred sighed mightily as he lay down by the fireplace. He was snoring in a matter of minutes. Wet and exhausted, Megan threw her waterlogged clothing in the laundry hamper and wrapped up in her velvety robe. This, too, had become a routine. But it was a comfortable one. She pulled the transcript from the top of the fridge, where she'd stored it in its envelope. Unfolding it, she repeated the word *tres* in her head, working to find a solution. It could mean so many things. Eventually, she just started rearranging the words, putting a few together and then trying another combination.

Always be with me... NO.
    Follow the storms... no.
    It's just behind me... no.
    Please be careful...

. . .

MEGAN STOPPED, REPEATING THE LAST PHRASE IN HER head. Then she spoke it out loud. "Please be careful." She straightened up from her slouching and tapped her finger on the page, counting from one word to the next. One, two, *three*... one, two *three*. "Oh my gosh," She pulled a highlighter from the small wooden cup that held various pens and pencils and began highlighting every third word in his message.

PLEASE. BE. CAREFUL. YOU. WILL. BE. IN. DANGER. FOLLOW. The. Rope. Behind. Edgewater. To. The. Beach. Below.

STUNNED, SHE SAT BACK IN HER CHAIR, STARING ACROSS THE room. He was giving her directions. Directions to something she assumed was significant to his case. A rope? Was she supposed to scale the cliffs? No wonder he said she'd be in danger. They were treacherous at the back of Edgewater Estates. It was what gave the upscale subdivision its million-dollar views, but it was also why they'd built an iron railing around the whole place.

She released a slow breath, wishing there was some way for her to ask him questions. If she were being honest, running out to a cliff face and sliding down a rope to the bottom wasn't something she was eager to do. But then, her curiosity was well-lit and smoldering away as she mused over just what Santiago might be hiding at the base of the cliffs.

A clap of thunder struck, and she flinched. It rolled across the sky and vibrated through her house, leaving her heart racing. She walked to the window to see another flash of lightning just before the rain began to fall. Storms came quickly when they traveled across the water. One minute it would be clear, and the next it was pouring rain and hail and anything else it could throw at you.

So, there would be no scaling cliffs today. Tomorrow was Sunday, so she could possibly explore then. But bright and early Monday morning, she was off to ask a Mr. Carter Dewald to beef up her investment portfolio. Really, it would be helpful anyway since her portfolio had stayed basically the same since the day she'd opened it ten years earlier.

There was a knock on the door, and Megan's eyes narrowed. She squinted through the dark, cloudy sky and heavy rain to see Kenneth's car. Slowly, she made her way to the door, glancing at the clock on her kitchen wall. It was only 2 p.m. and had barely been one hour since he left.

She opened the door to see him dripping wet and looking rather miserable. He grimaced as he looked back at her, although his dark brown eyes were rich and warm. She grinned. "Out enjoying the beautiful day, are you?"

A crack of thunder drowned out his answer, and she ushered him inside quickly. "Here, let me take this," Megan pulled the drenched coat from his shoulders and draped it across a barstool, letting it drip on the tile flooring. "It seems I'm always taking your coats, but this one I'll be sure to give back."

She winked and then noticed his eyes drop to the paper and highlighter on her counter. Snatching it away, she shoved both inside the manilla envelope and tossed it above the fridge again. "Just a puzzle I've been working on," she said.

Kenneth glanced at the fridge and then another clap of thunder shook through the house. "This is insane," he said, running his hands through his wet hair and causing a cascade of drips down his shirt. "I'm sorry. I was just coming back to say goodbye and then this storm hit." He shrugged. "I was hoping we could go for a walk together, but maybe staying inside would be a better idea."

His gaze was back, the one that had her heart warming. And the thought that he'd wanted to go on a walk with her was running on repeat in the back of her mind. Megan took two mugs out of the cupboard. "Well, both of those options sound good to me, but perhaps we should go with the one that doesn't have us both coming down with pneumonia." She scooped some cocoa in each and used the steam tap to fill them both with hot water. Sliding one to Kenneth, she handed him a spoon.

"Thank you, Ms. Henny," he said with a smile.

The color in his face had returned as he warmed up, and Megan couldn't help but enjoy it. The lightning still flashed outside, but the thunder had calmed down.

"I love storms," she said as she walked to the couch.

Kenneth responded with, "Mm."

But she wasn't sure if he was commenting on the storm or on his first sip of hot cocoa.

He followed her and settled down on the couch, staring into his cup as he stirred it. "You know," he said, "I've been thinking about your question earlier, and I knew I needed to come back."

Megan sipped her cocoa and waited, intrigued. Kenneth glanced at her and then turned back to the rain on the window. "Santiago has a history with his family." He shrugged. "He did rebel against their business before. I remember hearing about it, although I didn't know him at all back then. I hadn't even met his parents, but I knew the names Mark and Carolina Fitch just like the next person. Rumor had it their son wanted them to sell the business and become humanitarians, but he took a pretty extreme path in expressing that desire. It was during a high-profile showcase event for the company, and he stormed in, pushed tables over, spilled priceless jewelry on the floor." Kenneth shook his head. "It was quite a few years ago, so he was fairly young. And while I understand your friendship with him and your desire to help him out"—his gaze wandered from his cocoa cup to her eyes—"I just want you to know he's had a past. He's not squeaky clean. I'm not saying he's guilty, but we should probably just let this case run its course and try to support him however we can."

"Oh." Megan wasn't sure what to say. The fact that Santiago might possibly be guilty had been pushed from her mind the moment she decided to help him. But really, who had she spoken to except for Santiago and his lawyers? She took a long drink of cocoa, letting it soothe her nerves. Because even though Kenneth was likely trying to encourage her to leave the case alone, all it had done was solidify the need to talk to someone like Carter Dewald.

Chapter Nine

S unday it never stopped raining, leaving her to spend most of her time reading, and the rest of it feeling guilty for not finishing repairs around the house. She tried calling Derek, but he didn't answer, so she left a message and waited for a return call... which never came. But answer or not, first thing in the morning she was off to Seattle.

Monday came quickly. Fred laid his huge canine cranium on her lap, and Megan was glad she'd brought him along. She told herself it was for safety since she was traveling alone, but really she just loved to be with him. He was like a little kid on a vacation. How could she leave him out? She smoothed her hand over his ear where his fur was the softest. His eyes closed, and he sunk a little heavier on her leg.

Driving to Seattle a second time had her thinking more and more of her parents. She needed to stop in and say hello, even if it meant the inevitable chiding of her personal life choices. They were still her parents, and really, now that she was jobless and had zero income... maybe she should have listened to them.

She laughed out loud. A small stint of joblessness wasn't

going to change her love for the small seaside town of Seacrest. She scratched under Fred's ear. "We're happy, aren't we boy?" His tail smacked the seat next to her as he wagged it.

Her phone navigator, in a sexy English accent, directed her to the next exit. She took a slow breath, glancing in the backseat where her last-minute idea was in her small suitcase. She was second guessing her plans to wear a disguise. But really, if she wanted to do this completely incognito, a disguise was the best way to go. Still, she felt a rush of nerves imagining her black wig sliding off or her much too classy clothing looking out of place on her.

"Take the next left and your destination will be on the right," the sexy voice said.

She pulled into a gas station and parked. Her heart was racing, and she took a few breaths. It was no big deal, really. She had scheduled an appointment with Mr. Dewald that morning, and all she had to do was ask him a few questions and leave. She leaned forward and saw the edge of a building down the next road. It had to be the one. There were at least thirty floors, and the deep tint of the windows and smooth edges of the modern design were impressive. Definitely the place.

"Okay, Fred, give me just a minute." She cracked his window a few inches and pulled her luggage out, heading for the women's room.

When she'd made the change and stood looking back at herself in the foggy bathroom mirror, she adjusted the wig, pleased that it felt snug on her head. The tall boots weren't something she would wear normally, but she'd always prided herself in her ability to walk in heels. These tested her talents to the max, but at least they were more comfortable than she'd imagined. The skirt fit the look and her silk tank and beige leather jacket paired well.

With her suitcase stuffed full of her joggers and hoodie, she practiced her walk on the way out, catching a rather beguiled look from the cashier. He no doubt was wondering how he didn't notice her on the way in. She hurried to the car but stopped when Fred barked at her, baring his teeth.

"Fred," she said calmly, reaching her hand through the door. "It's me. Sorry for the strange new look." He sniffed her hand and wagged his tail, although he jumped back when her hair swung in his direction.

"Okay, let's do this." She lifted her chin and stepped on the gas pedal with the toe of her pointy boot.

Inside the building, the reception area was everything she might have expected to see in a multi-million-dollar company lobby. Shiny touches and expensive taste glimmered back at her from every hinge and window. She stepped into her role, modeling the classy, confident woman she was trying to portray. Her lips formed an easy smile at the man behind the reception counter. "I have an appointment at two," she said, her tone buttery smooth. The man hardly noticed and typed away on his computer.

"Ms. Sanders?" he asked, without looking up. She was using a name Derek had picked out.

"Yes,"

"Have a seat and we'll be right with you, ma'am." He glanced up just long enough to smile and then began typing again.

"Thank you." Megan settled in a chair, finding herself the only one among at least a dozen crushed-velvet wingback chairs. She crossed her legs and flipped through a yacht club magazine as the minutes ticked by.

Soon it had been close to an hour, and her feet were practically numb from her tight, pointy boots. She switched from one crossed leg to the other, wiggling her toes as much as she could.

"Ms. Sanders?" The young man who'd been seated at the reception desk was now standing aside it and holding a door open, gesturing to her. "Are you ready?"

Was she ready? If it had been any other office, she would have graced them with an appropriately sarcastic comment. But as it was, she simply nodded and attempted to stand on her numb feet. She adjusted the strap to her purse for a moment, giving her feet time to increase their blood flow before she began walking. She swayed a little on her way to the door but managed to stay mostly steady.

"Right this way." The clean-cut gentleman led her down a quiet hall and into another reception room. This one only had four chairs, and there was a single door next to them. "He'll be with you any moment now."

The man walked away, and she sighed before sitting down again, hoping it wouldn't be too much longer, or she'd have to take off her boots and carry them. And that might not give the impression she was going for. She wondered what Fred was up to, wagering he'd already taken a long nap and was now trying to shove his nose through the space between the lowered window and the doorframe.

The door to the office swung open, and a large man filled the entrance. He was a little round, but mostly he was tall, nearly touching the top frame of the door. His short brown hair was neat and his suit stylish. But it was his eyes that caught her attention. They were a beautiful taupe, mixed between gray and brown and overwhelmingly intense. He wasn't smiling and looked like a very sober person, but she made sure to act the part she'd begun over the phone.

Extending her hand, she flashed a full smile and shook his hand warmly. "So nice to meet you, Mr. Dewald. I'm glad you had an appointment available this afternoon. I thought for sure your schedule would be booked out for months."

"Yes." He pulled his hand from her grasp. "I'm happy to

hear there was a spot open as well. Usually, it's fairly difficult to schedule something so last minute."

She felt like she was being chided, and it had her panicking. In order to get someone like him talking, she'd have to be on his good side for sure.

"Oh, I am well aware of how busy you are," she complimented. "Someone with your reputation is hardly hurting for clients. Thank you so much for speaking with me today."

"Of course, Ms. Sanders." He sat down behind a bulky cherrywood desk.

"Please call me Elaine," she said politely, sitting down and crossing her legs yet again. She was already counting down the minutes until she could rip off her boots along with the sleek wig that was beginning to itch.

"Elaine."

It looked like he had attempted to smile, but all she'd noticed was a quick twitch in his cheeks. She smiled back, anyway.

"You have your portfolio here?" He reached a thick-fingered hand in her direction.

"Oh." Megan adjusted in her seat. "No, I emailed it over last night, as your assistant recommended. Did you not receive it?" Derek had made up a fake portfolio, assuring it was imperfect and realistic to her age and situation.

His hand thumped against the desktop, and he turned to a laptop open next to him, typing quickly. "Let me see here." He continued typing and clicking.

"I've actually been searching for the right partnership"— Megan glanced around the room—"and really wanted to take a minute to get a feel for your company and perhaps a little background on you if that's okay?"

She glanced back when he stopped typing and tried to remain calm, looking into his dead-faced stare.

"Get a feel for it?" he repeated, his eyes narrowing.

Megan forced another smile onto her lips, stopping herself from licking them. "Yes. I really like to connect with the people I work with. It means a lot to me when I know them a little more personally. Don't you agree?"

He shrugged, his round shoulders lifting his suit impressively. "It's not necessary, but I suppose we have a minute." He glanced at the screen of his laptop. "Our internet was out for a time, and the document is just now loading."

"Wonderful." Megan could tell he was going to need a little bit of a lead-in if he were ever to start talking. "I hear congratulations are in order." She leaned forward slightly, smiling. "You're engaged?"

Mr. Dewald's intriguing eyes hardened. "How did you hear about that?" he asked in a graveled voice. Megan thought back to the news article she'd read, realizing it was more of a tabloid opinion piece than actual news.

She cleared her throat. "Well, when I researched the company, I came across an article about it."

He seemed to appreciate her answer, and he nodded slowly. "Yes, there has been some speculation on the date. I hoped for a ceremony in a matter of weeks, but my Lyanna is a special woman. She wants everything just right." A smile flickered across his face, and he lifted one hand up. "And so, I try to oblige when I can."

The way he spoke had Megan wondering which undesirable family members this Lyanna wanted removed before the wedding picture. Mr. Dewald glanced at his computer screen as if he were ready to move on from the getting to know you.

"And how did you two meet?" Megan asked.

She knew the moment she'd spoken that it was somehow going too far. Mr. Dewald didn't answer right away, looking back at her dryly.

"That's a story for another time," he said, swiveling in his seat. "Now, looking at your portfolio here." His lips twisted a little as if he'd clenched his teeth. "I can see that there's been a mistake." He paused to stare back at her, his expression more serious than before. "We deal with businesses looking to grow or merge their companies, not with private retirement accounts."

"Oh, I'm so sorry." Megan was scrambling, trying to think of a way to get him talking again. "Has your company ever dealt with accounts like mine?"

His eyes flashed to the computer screen and looked very unimpressed when they returned to her. "No."

Attempting to look flustered was easy with the way her heart had begun to race. "Well, is there a business close by you could refer me to? I've taken the day off to get this settled." His expression didn't change, and she wondered if he could see right through her.

"There are several down the street you could contact." He sighed and glanced at his watch. "I suggest simply walking in and trying to get a spot if today is what you're hoping for." He stood from his chair and held his hand out, and Megan followed suit, tipping a little on one of her high heels as she did. She shook his hand and thanked him. Turning to leave, she concentrated as much as possible on walking quickly and steadily, as if she were born wearing boots up to her knees. She managed to get the heavy door open and squeeze through without falling.

Once she was out in the empty lobby, she paused, defeated. Here she'd come all the way to Seattle to talk to Mr. Dewald and hadn't gotten anything out of it.

Another man in a suit approached her. "Are you looking for someone, ma'am?"

His voice was more intimidating than she was prepared for. She brushed her sleek black hair back. "Actually, I spoke with Mr. Dewald and was just leaving."

Another man appeared in the hall, and Megan nearly

gasped at the sight of Kenneth. He froze when he saw her, his face slack and eyes widening. He looked terrified. But in the next moment, he'd wiped the expression away. With one last, quick glance, he continued down the hall and out of sight without a word.

The man in front of her glanced back, noticing her distraction. Megan stepped around him. "I'd better be going —" she started, but the man moved in front of her quickly, blocking her way.

"Allow me to escort you," he said. Without waiting for an answer, he turned and began walking.

Irritated, Megan wanted to refuse. It was clear he was suspicious and just wanted to keep an eye on her. When he turned down another hall too quickly, he nearly ran into an older couple, and he spun out of their way. For a moment his suit coat flared out, revealing a black pistol strapped to his waist.

Megan felt a sudden wave of cold shock jolt through her. The reality that she could be in some very deep trouble was tugging at her mind, but she didn't know what she could possibly have done to merit a threat. He continued leading her, and she tried to remember which colorless, bare hallway she'd come from on her way in. It seemed like they were walking for too long, that perhaps they'd passed the main entrance already and were headed elsewhere.

A door opened in the hall. The room inside was a kitchen, buzzing with conversation and the sound of dishes clanking. A woman stepped out, chatting with someone even as she left.

"I wasn't the one who ordered two cheesecakes—oh." She sidestepped to avoid them both. Megan smiled quickly at the woman, hoping to encourage an introduction and perhaps a long conversation. "I'm so sorry," the woman said, giving Megan's mysterious companion a sly smile. Taking a step closer, she bumped him with her hip. "I keep running into you."

The man stepped away and dipped his head quickly. "Miss Bellerose."

"Oh, stop that." She giggled. "Call me Lyanna." Her hair was blonde and wavy, reaching to her shoulders, and her dark eyes were big and beautiful. She had a slender mouth and delicate chin that matched her very small nose. Overall, she had a unique type of beauty that was enchanting.

The man turned back to Megan, and she could see his face was slightly flushed. "Let's go," he demanded.

"And who are you?" Lyanna shoved her hand between them, and Megan took it quickly, grateful for this boisterous woman.

"I just met with a man who I hear is your fiancé?" Megan let her eyes fill with excitement even when she was still nauseous knowing there was a gun one foot away from her. "Congratulations," she continued, her voice cracking.

Lyanna didn't seem to notice. Her face broke into a thrilled smile at the mention of her fiancé. "Did he tell you that?" She nearly squealed. "How exciting. Usually he's so tight-lipped, no one can get a word out of him. Unless of course, you're talking about investing. Now *that* is something he can go on about forever." Lyanna glanced from Megan's face to the man next to her. "Are you a client, then?" she asked.

"No, unfortunately." Megan's knees were shaking, and she shifted her weight. "I'm still looking for the right fit."

"Well, good!" Lyanna linked her arm with Megan's. "That means we're free to go to lunch together." She eyed the man again. "Thanks for your help, but I'll take it from here." She spun Megan around with a giggle and pulled the door to the kitchen open. "We're going to get some lunch."

Megan was so relieved to have an escape, she could have

kissed the woman who now had a hold on her wrist and was dragging her through a very nice chef's kitchen. She glanced back just before the door closed behind them to see the man with the gun hadn't moved. He stood watching them, his eyes boring into hers until the door swung closed.

Chapter Ten

Megan breathed a sigh of relief.

"They can be pretty intense, can't they?" Lyanna said, dropping a little of her enthusiasm although it still sparkled in her eyes. "Sorry about that. Security is a top priority here, although if you ask me it's a little overdone. I mean, c'mon, there aren't hundreds of spies sneaking around."

"Heh." Megan forced out as much of a laugh as she could. "Yeah, crazy."

"What, was Kyle heading off to interrogate you?" Lyanna burst out laughing. "Can you imagine?"

They came to a small diner, and Lyanna lifted one hand, signaling to the maître d' before pulling out a chair at one of the tables. "Here, let's have lunch. I'm sorry you can't do business with my fiancé, but actually I'm glad because that means we can talk about him all you want." She giggled and sat down, and Megan sat in the chair next to her.

"Thank you, I appreciate it. My name is Elaine Sanders." Megan shook Lyanna's hand again, feeling like their previous introduction was too rushed. "I'm sure the man I was with meant no harm, but yes." She widened her eyes. "He was intense for sure."

"As the fiancée of the boss, let me just say food will fix everything." Lyanna signaled again, and a young woman came to their table. "Two iced lemonades please."

The woman nodded and rushed away. Lyanna turned back to Megan. "It might not sound like much, but just wait and see how they've recreated an old country picnic favorite."

"Thank you," Megan said, wondering if Lyanna might know anything about Santiago. But how would she steer the conversation that way without raising suspicion? Especially after showing up with a security guard... or whatever that guy had been. She ran one hand through her silky, black hair. "I meant to ask," she started, hoping to get her new friend talking. "When are you two getting married?"

"Oh, I hope soon." Lyanna was digging through her purse and didn't look up. "There are just a few things we need to situate first, and I'm not sure how long it will take. I'd love to get married tomorrow, but..."

She zipped her purse and set it on the table, although Megan never saw her retrieve anything. Lyanna's constant grin faded, widening her big eyes even more. Her gaze drilled into Megan's until she couldn't look away.

"Let me tell you a story," Lyanna said quietly, crossing her arms on the table and leaning forward.

Megan nodded. Lyanna's tone sounded intriguingly top secret.

"There's a legend from long ago. A story of Cleopatra and Marc Antony, each master of their own universe. They met one evening, intending a union of their cultures." Lyanna's long lashes fluttered, and she looked into Megan's eyes. "They sat together, and Cleopatra wore earrings made of the largest pearls in the world, said to have mystical properties. In the course of the evening, she removed one of the earrings. She took the pearl from its casing and dropped it into a glass half-full of vinegar, where it fizzed, dissolving completely. And then she drank it. With this ritual, it is said she solidified their love and immortalized her power."

The waitress returned, placing their drinks in front of them. Lyanna leaned back in her chair but didn't take her eyes off Megan.

As soon as the waitress left, she continued, "The pearl from her remaining earring was paired in a necklace of the finest dark pearls in history and has been fought over for centuries. It is said one knows this necklace by the number of pearls it holds. With Cleopatra consuming one, the necklace was constructed using only 84 pearls instead of the traditional 85." Lyanna's eyes finally strayed from Megan's, and she took a sip of her lemonade.

Megan hadn't even taken the time to look at their drinks, but now she lifted the beautiful glass in her hand. The rim was piled with fruits and sugar-covered lemon slices on one side, and the lemonade swirled with red and pink coloring. Crushed strawberries filled the bottom. She took a sip, closing her eyes at the sweet, tangy flavor.

"What did I tell you?" Lyanna smiled, taking the straw in her lips again.

"It's incredible," Megan agreed. "And that story, is it supposed to be true?"

Lyanna smiled, tilting her head so that her blonde hair trailed down her arm. "It's absolutely true. At least, it always has been for me. I was told that story when I was very young. My existence was dark, but *this*..." She stirred the drink in her hand, looking into it as if mesmerized. "This legend saved my life. It revived my soul and gave me hope. I had nothing, but I spoke to the moon and stars and dreamed of Cleopatra's necklace. And one day I will have it." Lyanna's face slowly darkened.

It was a look that gave Megan chills. "But why would you need it?" she asked. "Your fiancé is abounding with financial security."

Lyanna's eyes flickered back to Megan. "It's not about money, Elaine. Money is cold and uncaring and cruel. It's about the universe and powers that direct our lives in deeper ways than material things every could. I told Carter that the day he finds it is the day we marry." She set her drink down. "He tells me he's working on it, but I've given him a deadline, and after that, I move back to France. It may sound harsh, but I'm a Libra. I need to have balance in my life. I've dreamed about the pearls of Cleopatra since I was a child..." She paused, looking out across the tables.

"But, what if it doesn't exist? What if it was just a story?" Megan asked, feeling sorry for poor Mr. Dewald.

"If it doesn't exist"—her gaze was frozen, staring right through Megan—"then I've been misled in the deepest, most spiritual way." She brushed her fingertips along her face slowly, as if in a trance, sweeping her hair back.

"And what has Carter done to retrieve them?" Megan asked. "What is he willing to do?"

A moment of silence passed between them before Lyanna answered, "He would do anything." Her eyes settled, calm and yet menacing. "Absolutely anything."

Megan felt a sudden wave of uneasiness and stirred her drink, wondering how many pearls were on the necklace she had. The one Fred had found from somewhere.

"Oh my gosh," Megan stood suddenly, nearly toppling her chair over. "Fred."

"Who?" Lyanna jumped up as well, placing one hand on Megan's shoulder. "Are you okay?"

"He's my dog—Fred. I forgot all about him. He's out in the car." Megan scooted her chair in. "I'm sorry, we'll have to do lunch another time?"

"Of course," Lyanna said, although her spirits seemed to have plummeted. Her bubbly personality was gone, leaving a hollowness to her gaze.

Megan stopped, turning to this new friend who she could easily imagine as an enemy. But what she couldn't imagine was balancing the threat of breaking up with a fiancée for something as far-fetched as the necklace of Cleopatra. Something that was most likely a legend. A myth. But something told her Lyanna hadn't grown up with a clear division between real and fantasy.

She looked into Lyanna's eyes and rested her hands on the beautiful woman's slender arms. "I feel like I need to caution you, Lyanna." She glanced across her face, trying to portray the concern she felt. "Balance in life can also mean letting go of an obsession and accepting love imperfectly."

Lyanna took a quick step back, her posture rigid, and her eyes flashing with anger. "Goodbye, Elaine," she said. "I'm glad we met, and maybe we will see each other again."

Megan wondered what Lyanna would say, or what she might do, if she knew Megan could have her necklace. It was impossible, of course. But something told Megan her life would be worth much less in her new friend's eyes if she suspected the necklace were Cleopatra's... and her future husband had the power to make anything happen. Indeed, he was Marc Antony.

"Maybe we will," Megan said, smiling. But the gesture was not returned. Lyanna's beauty was frozen in place. Only her eyes followed Megan as she walked away.

The moment she stepped outside of the small dining area, Megan looked out on a long hall and the exit foyer beyond. But just in front of it was the same man who'd tried escorting her out before. The one Lyanna called Kyle. He turned the moment their eyes met, walking toward her and speaking into a handheld device.

With her heart pounding, Megan planned to walk right out the door. What choice did she have? The building was a maze. She forced an easy smile on her face and plodded ahead in her tall boots, chin lifted, shoulders back. Cowering under this man's gaze wasn't an option. But he was quicker than she thought, meeting her when she'd only traveled halfway down the hall. Darn her pointy heeled boots. Her legs shook as she fought the urge to run for the door.

"Ma'am," he said, reaching for her arm.

"What is this?"

They both spun around to see Kenneth coming out of the dining room. He had a wide smile on his face and shook his head as he approached. "What are the odds," he practically shouted, hugging her quickly. "And here I thought you'd already left for Chicago."

Megan was too stunned to respond. She just stared back at him, trying to get her sluggish brain to catch up to whatever he was doing.

"I'm glad you took my recommendation to heart," he said, glancing at the man who still had a hand outstretched as if he were going to grab Megan at any second. He turned to Megan again. "Dewald Agency is the very best."

"Y-yes," Megan finally said, "they really are impressive. But I'm afraid I misunderstood their services." She glanced at the stranger briefly as if he were merely another friend in the conversation. "I need someone for personal investing, not business or commercial."

"Oh," Kenneth slapped his forehead dramatically. "I'm so sorry, that's my fault. Here, let me point out where you need to go." He draped his arm around her back, leading her down the hall.

"Wait, Mr. Bradburn," The man took a quick step forward as if he were going to try to stop them.

Kenneth dropped the smile and any pleasantness his

features held before. Instead, he became wholly intimidating as he looked back at the man. "Yes, Kyle?"

"Well, I just..." the man stuttered a bit, finally dropping his objection with a wave of his hand. "Have a good day."

"You as well." Kenneth returned his attention to Megan. "Now as I was saying, it's just a few buildings down from this one." He walked with her, keeping his arm around her back. But when they got to the glass doors, he leaned to the side and pointed, as if picking out the building. "My car is parked in the side lot. It's self-driving. I'll unlock it from here. Just get in, and I'll program the coordinates. Plate number t-o-y-1-2."

"But—"

"It was wonderful seeing you again," he said, his voice echoing slightly in the high ceilings. He patted her on the back and began walking away. He turned back as he went, giving her a toothy smile. "Enjoy your time in Seattle."

"Thank you," she said, catching sight of Kyle and two additional men coming around the corner. She spun around and pushed the door open. What was even going on? Was Kenneth being overly suspicious, or was he saving her life? She could imagine both very clearly, but the image of being tied up and thrown in a trunk was winning over her imagination. Hurrying out to the lot, she couldn't leave Fred behind. But executing whatever escape Kenneth had given her might be more difficult with him at her heels.

It was no matter.

She unlocked the car on her way over and wrenched the door open. "C'mon Fred," She clipped his leash and slammed the door, locking it again as she hurried to the side lot. The door to the building opened just as she slipped around the side. She pulled on the leash, running as much as she could in heels. There were sounds of voices behind her, and she hurried to scan the few cars in the lot. Each space was marked as private parking, and in the last row, she saw the license plate. TOY12. It stopped her in her tracks. A pearly-gray sports car like she'd never seen before.

The car engine started, and she jumped, hurrying to the driver's side. She pulled the door open and let Fred in, diving in quickly behind him.

"Please, buckle up," the car said in a soothing, kind voice.

She clawed at the seatbelt and jammed it in the buckle.

"Please, buckle up."

"I did!" she shouted, seeing Marcus and the two men coming toward her. One of them pointed, and the men began to run.

"Please, buckle up."

"Oh—Fred!" Megan shouted, pulling the passenger's side seatbelt around him quickly. The car started forward just as someone pounded on her window. She screamed, throwing her hands over her head.

"Stop the car!" The man shouted.

Megan choked off another scream and ducked down as he made a fist and punched the window. Suddenly, the car tires squealed, peeling out of the lot. Fred barked, dancing on his feet as he tried to steady himself in the fast-moving car.

Megan was gasping. She slowly rose from where she'd been huddled and looked back to see the men watching her drive away. The tinting was dark, so they might not have known it was her. They never exactly said a name. But why in the world were they angry enough to punch a window? Her head was spinning, and she felt a wave of nausea. She placed her cool palms on her cheeks, closing her eyes as they turned a corner. It was nice to let the car do the escaping for her. She didn't care that she had no idea where they were going.

Hopefully Kenneth chose well. She thought of her little red hatchback, wondering what they might do with it. Maybe they didn't know it was hers, and they'd leave it alone. Or if they did, maybe she'd never see it again. Was it Lyanna who'd sent them after her? She'd seemed so friendly at first and then...

Fred barked and her head pounded, making her nauseous again. "It's okay," she said, trailing her hand down his back. "We're okay."

She swallowed hard, trying to settle her turning stomach. She shook when she thought about what could have happened. If Kenneth hadn't warned her, and she'd been in her little hatchback, she wouldn't have peeled out of the parking lot. She would have been polite and waited when they called for her. She would have tried to talk to them. And when they punched it, the window would have smashed easily. They would have gotten to her... and then what?

She shivered.

All this because she wanted to find out more about Santiago and the case. Well, now she knew he was in with some risky clients. For once, she found herself taking the blame off of his parents and turning it instead to his clients. Maybe his parents simply knew what he was in for, and jail was a protection for him.

"We've reached your destination," the car said as they pulled through an electronic gate. It closed behind them, and they came to a stop in a wide stone courtyard. "Have a pleasant day."

The car engine turned off, and the doors unlocked. Megan noticed she'd been squeezing the leash in both hands, and she loosened her grip, looking out at a modern mansion. "Wow," she breathed. "We might be safe here."

Chapter Eleven

Megan took a moment to calm down. Rubbing Fred's ears, she rested her forehead against his, her black wig hanging around him. "Good boy," she said, still feeling guilty about leaving him in the car for so long.

Her eyes flew open. "I bet you have to go." With one look at the impressive landscaping, she cringed. "I'll make sure to clean it up later. C'mon,"

Opening the door, she got a full look at the building in front of them, and her mouth dropped open. The leash zipped through her hands as Fred bounded off to a green stretch of grass under the trees, but she hardly noticed. She couldn't look away from the estate. It had two levels above ground and looked to possibly have one below. There were three gorgeous stone chimneys that matched the red and tan stones of the courtyard. The building was clad with vertical slate gray concrete and had rich wood beams and pillars in the front. The effect was sleek and ageless. She doubted he'd left it open, but found herself walking up the steps, anyway.

She was delighted when the front door obliged with a twist of her hand, and she stepped inside. Glancing behind her, she saw the gate was closed, and the grounds were surrounded by a massive stone wall crusted with ivy. Fred would be in heaven.

"I'll be inside!" she called, leaving the door open a crack so he could nose his way in if he wanted.

Her heart was still racing from running for her life. It was surreal, the way those men had pursued her. What kind of threat was she, anyway?

She walked slowly through the house, across polished stone floors and long-haired rugs. The entryway led to a grand living area with deep cedar beams and a massive fireplace with white birch logs stacked beside it. Everything was immaculate, clean, and tasteful. It smelled like leather and timber, and she breathed it in, gazing out the windows to the grounds beyond. A hillside stretched out behind the house, littered with trees, giving it a rural feel in the middle of urban life. Fred ran across her view, tongue out and legs pumping.

It felt strange to be in Kenneth's home. Or one of his homes. He had to have at least a few. But there wasn't anything to give additional clues about him, no guitar in the corner or books left open on the table. All she could see was that he had good taste. Or at least, his interior designer and custom builder did.

She wandered quietly past the fireplace and down the hall to the back of the house. For the first time, she came to a picture on the wall. It showed what looked like Kenneth's family. He was easy to spot on the center left side of the photo, standing next to who she assumed were his parents. They smiled, each with dark hair and brown eyes like Kenneth. His cousin Estelle was there too, along with a few other couples she didn't recognize, and young children scattered about. He'd mentioned he was an only child, so it must have been a photo of some of the extended family. A few of the people she didn't recognize resembled Estelle in different ways.

There was another hall jutting deeper into the building, and she continued on, discovering a master bedroom at the end. It was secluded and quiet, with another fireplace and a cozy sitting area in one corner. The bed was huge and layered with blankets and pillows. On the nightstand, there was a notebook with a pen left on top as if he'd written in it recently. As curious as she was, she didn't open it. She only paced the room, admiring a luxurious set of slippers and a bookshelf that held nothing but fantasy and science fiction novels.

She picked one off the shelf, flipping through it and smiling. Somehow, she'd thought his personal library would be full of non-fiction business titles. There were even a few romance books at the bottom of one shelf.

A door slammed, and she gasped, dropping the book. She spun around and hurried out, suddenly terrified that the men had followed her there.

"Megan?"

Kenneth's voice echoed through the house, loud and afraid. The sound of Fred's claws on the stone accompanied him, and she sighed with relief, going back to the living room to see Kenneth skid to a stop at the sight of her.

"Oh my gosh," he said, gasping. Sweat was gathered along his hairline, and he leaned forward with his hand on the kitchen counter. "You made it." He was breathing hard, and he brought one hand to his chest, closing his eyes with a sigh.

"I have no idea what happened back there," Megan explained.

He only nodded and pulled her into a hug, wig and all. His

chest rose and fell with his breath, pressing against her. It was alarming to see him so worried, as if her life really were in danger.

She stepped out of his arms slowly, eyeing him. "Kenneth, what's going on?" Fred trotted by happily in the background, disappearing down a side hall.

Kenneth took her hand and led her to the couch behind them, sitting down silently for a moment. He held a hand up, as if his answer needed steadying.

"Why..." He shook his head, looking back at her with wide eyes. "*Why* would you meet with Carter Dewald?"

His fear was pricking at her from the inside, and suddenly anger flared up from down deep. "Because I wanted to," she retorted, pulling her wig off with one hand. "Why not? Santiago is stuck in jail and his parents... I don't know, they're attacking him for something he never did."

"And what's that?" Kenneth asked, his head tilting in the silence that followed. "What did he do exactly? What did they accuse him of? What laws have been broken?"

Megan glanced across the room, feeling increasingly foolish. But when she turned back to Kenneth, her anger melted away. "You're right. I don't know how to answer that except to say I felt like no one's trying. Like he's just being left in a jail when he could be cleared. But he asked me for help. So"— she shrugged—"I wanted to go and pretend to be a client. I had no idea it would be a business that practiced martial law and had psychotic security guards. How could I?"

"I know." He shook his head, one hand resting on her knee. "It's crazy."

"And, by the way..." Megan's lips twisted into a rigid smile. "Why do you do business there?"

He stood, pacing the room. "Well, because they're known for being the best. My family has done business with them on the East Coast for a long time. So, when I started up a few business ventures out here in the West, it was only natural to go with them." He ran a hand through his outgrown hair. "But now, I might be rethinking that decision."

"Yeah, you might want to." Megan took a slow breath, still trying to calm down.

Fred returned from his exploration of the house with a shoe in his mouth. "Oh no, Fred." Megan moved to get up.

"No, it's okay," Kenneth said, watching as Fred laid down on the carpet and began chewing his new treasure. "Those are old, anyway. I don't mind."

Megan doubted that. The shoes looked practically new. But she left him to it, sinking back into the couch cushions. Outside the windows, the sun was beginning to hang low in the sky. "I don't know how I'm going to get my car after all that."

Kenneth sat down next to her with a sly grin. "Actually, you don't need to worry about it. I drove your car over here."

"You drove my little car *here*? To your mansion?" Megan laughed, wishing she could have seen it.

"It's not a mansion," he said, glancing around with a shrug. His gaze returned to her, and he nodded. "And yes, I assumed that's why you left the keys on the seat." He smiled. "I see why you bought it. It feels like secret beach turnouts and sandy back roads."

"Doesn't it?" She looked back at him, enjoying the differences in their lives and the similarities in their tastes. "I love your house, by the way." She closed her eyes. "It's so comfortable. But I really should get on the road and head back to Seacrest, unless I want to be driving all night... which I don't."

"If you want to stay here tonight, there's a guest room down the front hall,"

She looked back at Kenneth, feeling chaotic inside. His

lips flickered into a smile and he stood, walking to the kitchen. "But if you really need to get on the road, at least let me make you some dinner." He took his coat off and draped it across the back of a barstool. Unbuttoning the cuffs of his shirt, he rolled up one and then the other.

Megan sighed, feeling too exhausted to get up. She untied the knot her hair had been in all day and shook it out. Next, she pulled her boots off, sinking back into the couch in relief. "I'd love that." She closed her eyes. "But don't go to too much trouble. A sandwich is fine."

"Ok." There were sounds of drawers opening and cabinet doors closing. "Go ahead and rest for a few minutes, and I'll let you know when it's ready."

"Thanks," she mumbled, pulling a throw of some kind from the back of the couch. It was as soft as cashmere, and she hoped it wasn't just for show as she draped it over herself and listened to the sound of something sizzling in a pan. She meant to tell him again that he was going to too much trouble, but her drowsiness quickly took over, and she fell asleep.

The next thing she knew, someone said her name. Her eyes opened slowly to see Kenneth kneeling down in front of her with his hand on her shoulder.

"Are you hungry?" he asked quietly, as if the option of going back to sleep were still open. Both sounded wonderful, but now that she was awake, her stomach ached with hunger. She pushed off the couch and glanced at the table to see two plates set.

"Smells amazing," she said as she stumbled to her feet and followed him to the table. Each breath had her mouth watering. "Wow."

He pulled a chair out for her, and she sat, looking down at a plate with pasta, herb-crusted chicken, and a medley of steamed vegetables drizzled in a creamy white sauce. "This looks incredible," she said, waiting for him to take his seat next to her.

"Thank you," he said, sounding content.

The awkwardness that had seemed wedged between them at the event at Seacrest had vanished, although every now and then she could see a hesitance in his gaze. It was like he was gauging her, measuring when would be the right time to spring a bout of bad news. She twirled her fork in the pasta and stabbed a few vegetables as she thought. He began to eat as well, and gradually, she relaxed. A warm meal in her stomach definitely helped.

"I've been wanting to speak to you about a couple of things," Kenneth said. He pulled his napkin from his lap and wiped his mouth.

Oh boy.

It sounded like something serious. Megan tried to appear innocently interested, although her eyes were darting across his face, inspecting every flicker of expression. After scrutinizing him for far too long, she forced herself to look away, and that was when she saw the clock. "Oh my goodness, I'm going to get home so late," she said, spearing the last bite of chicken and plunging it into her mouth.

"Ah, well." Kenneth's face was a little red. "It can wait then, I mean, if you have to get going." He stood, scooting his chair in, although there was still half a meal on his plate. Megan glanced down at her own plate, feeling a little too much like a pig as it was practically licked clean.

"My offer still stands if you'd rather leave in the morning," Kenneth said. "I saw that there was a suitcase in the back of your car if that's what you're worried about. Looks like you'd have your things if you needed them."

Megan took a moment to think. Her parents were still on vacation, and after being harassed by a terrifying company, she wanted to run home as quickly as possible. But was that really necessary? Driving home this late would have her fighting drowsiness the whole way. The thought was misery. She looked back at Kenneth, who'd settled in his seat again and was awaiting her response with a kind smile. "Actually, that would be nice," she finally said.

Something clattered to the floor behind them, and she turned around to see Fred snatching up a book from the ground.

"Now *that*, I'll have to put a stop to," Kenneth said, standing again. "It's one of my favorites."

Fred took one look at him and lowered his head, peering back like he didn't agree. Megan got to her feet as well.

"I'm sorry, let me get it." She inched over to Fred, taking the book and ordering him to drop it. His eyes shifted from her to Kenneth, but after repeating the order, Megan was rewarded with a partly slobbered book.

Fred didn't move, standing with his head down and keeping his eyes on Kenneth. "I don't think he likes me yet," Kenneth said, taking the book Megan handed him and heading to the kitchen. He wiped it down between glances at Fred.

Megan felt a rush of relief at being able to stay at Kenneth's instead of driving home, alone and in the dark. She looked back at him to see he'd placed the book on the counter and was still staring at Fred.

"What was it you wanted to talk about?" she asked.

Kenneth abandoned his staring contest and returned to the table, taking a sip of sparkling cider. "Well, I was just worried, I guess." His eyes flickered to hers, and then he distracted himself with the view of his backyard full of climbing ivy and willow trees.

"When we were in Seacrest at the fundraiser, it felt a little strained... between us, I mean. And I understand that," he said, lifting his fork and moving his food around, although he didn't take a bite. "I understand I travel around a lot, and it's not really the kind of life very many people would be interested in." He sighed and set his fork down.

Megan's head was spinning. She'd assumed he wanted to keep their relationship at arm's length, but it didn't sound like that was what he was telling her. But then, her eyes scanned something on his counter, and all her focus vanished.

"What's that?" she asked, her gaze falling on a manilla envelope. She could only see part of the writing, but it looked identical to the one she'd received from Santiago's lawyer.

Kenneth looked up from his plate and then back at the envelope. "The mail. I just brought it in." Megan stood, and he pushed away from the table, watching her. "Is something wrong?" he asked.

She lifted the envelope, letting a few letters and flyers slide off the top. Kenneth stood next to her, reaching for it, once the label had been revealed. "This is from Santiago's lawyer," he said.

"Yes." Megan looked into his face, knowing she couldn't ask to read it. But the questions burned in her mind. What would Santiago send to Kenneth? Had he given up on waiting for her help and had decided to send the message to someone else? Or was it something entirely new? She wanted to snatch the envelop out of his hands and tear it open. But instead, she returned to the table and cleared her plate, taking the dishes to the sink while sneaking glances at him. He tapped the corner of the envelope on the counter while his eyes stared across the room.

Then suddenly, he slid one finger under the seal and popped it open, looking inside. Megan stared back at him, mesmerized, as she fumbled for the faucet and turned the water off distractedly. He reached his hand in and appeared to be flipping through pages, a few at least. Megan's curiosity was practically screaming. She could tell he was reading, although he never removed anything. Before she had the chance to ask, he left. She watched him walk swiftly down the hall and heard something from the back bedroom.

When he returned the envelope was gone. Whatever he'd just learned from Santiago, it was very clear... he didn't plan to share it with her.

Chapter Twelve

Megan rolled over in bed. It was still early morning, and light filtered through the sheer curtains gently. The room Kenneth had given her was gorgeous, of course. The fabrics and bedding were luxuriously soft and practically brand new. Everything was mostly white, with a bamboo side table and picture frames and a few splashes of sea-green accents. It was easy to imagine staying in bed half the day. But her mind wouldn't be still.

Last night had started out comfortable, but that wasn't how it had ended. After Kenneth stowed away the envelope, any conversation had been Megan's doing. He'd been severely preoccupied. She did feel guilty about cutting off their conversation the second she'd seen the envelope, but she couldn't say if he'd been upset about that or about the contents. It had made Megan's curiosity even harder to deal with. But somehow, she'd managed not to ask him directly about the envelope, even though he had to know how desperately she wanted him to talk about it.

She slid out of bed and stood at the window. There was a blanket of fog across the yard, seeming to quiet the world.

Growing up, she'd become accustomed to the foggy mornings of Seattle. Something about it made her miss her parents, and she felt a new wave of guilt at the fact that they'd gone to Hawaii, and she didn't even know. What kind of daughter was she? But then, it would be easy to turn the tables around and ask what kind of parents would leave without talking to her?

She sighed, unlocking the screen of her cell and selecting their profile picture. It had been taken just a few years earlier and was very like them. Smiling and poised. They were always so picture perfect, but somehow it fit them. They tried very hard to be the kind, caring individuals they were seen as. Maybe it was why they couldn't see anything wrong in Jarron. He put on the pretty face, but there was definitely a menacing side beneath. A sliver of forgiveness made its way into her heart, and she realized she hadn't fully given them a chance to understand her situation.

Pushing the call button, she held the phone to her ear and waited through a few dial tones. Her father answered in a cheery voice, very much like himself. She hinted to Hawaii, and they were all apologies, her mother chiming in from the background. "It was your father's idea," she teased, both of them laughing the way vacationers do. Megan smiled. "It sounds wonderful. I'm glad you were able to get away. Do you need me to stop by the house? I'm in town for just a couple of days."

"You are?" Her mom must have stolen the phone because her voice was the only one now. "Well, why didn't you tell us? I'd love to spend the day with my daughter. We could go shopping and get ice cream, maybe stop by the bookstore."

"Mom, that sounds wonderful, but you don't have to come back from Hawaii just for me." Megan laughed. "I have a car now, so I can spend a weekend with you anytime you want."

There was a small pause. "And how's your business doing in Seacrest?"

Her mother's tone was a little nervous, but that was understandable seeing as how they had an almost-argument about it during their last call. That was the extent of their anger—*almost arguments*. It made Megan smile to realize again that she was raised by some very good people. But somehow, it hadn't rubbed off on her quite like she figured it should have. She'd been in plenty of *real* arguments.

"It's going good," she said, shrugging at her reflection in the window. "Money will be tight for a little while, but I expected that. I don't have many expenses, so it's okay."

"Oh, I'm glad to hear that," her mother said. Her father's voice called from the background, "We're proud of you, honey,"

"Yes, we are," her mother repeated. "We're so proud of you. I know you can make this work, if it's what you really want."

It felt so good to hear them say those words. Megan reveled in the glow of their support for a moment. A small tap sounded on her door, and she turned around.

"Come in."

Kenneth peeked in, looking freshly woken. His hair was disheveled and his face tired. He seemed to suddenly notice her phone, and he held a finger to his lips, whispering, "Do you want to go on a walk before breakfast?"

She smiled and nodded back at him. "One minute."

"Hey, Mom and Dad." She turned back to the window, and there was the sound of her door latching as Kenneth closed it again. "I'm going to be back on the road here in just a little while. Do you want me to stop by the house first? Just to check on things?"

"Uh..." Her mother sounded distracted. Megan listened to the sound of a car door closing and then a gust of wind in the phone. There was the distinct rushing sound of the ocean as well, and she closed her eyes, wishing she was there.

"Are you guys at the beach?" she asked.

"Yes dear, sorry." Her mother knew her well. "I'd love for you to stop by the house, thank you. Jarron's checking on things here and there, but it would be nice to have you stop in as well. We haven't changed the code yet, so just use that to get in and to power off the alarm."

"I will. Love you guys," Megan said.

"Oh honey, we love you so much."

She hung up the phone with a sigh. Somehow the ache of missing her parents had only multiplied after calling them, but the happiness of hearing their support was something entirely new. Something she was very grateful for.

As she dressed and headed out onto the classy sidewalks of Kenneth's neighborhood, it was strange the way things had shifted overnight. Suddenly it felt awkward to bring up their conversations from the day before, as if his decision not to share the contents of the envelope had changed them. It had hurt her feelings that he'd chosen not to confide in her.

What would Santiago have to say to Kenneth that he couldn't say to her, anyway? It wasn't making sense. But whatever it was, she was going to follow the directions in Santiago's message the moment she got home. If that was what he'd told Kenneth, that he'd gotten tired of waiting on her, she wanted to be the one to complete the task first.

She wound the leash around her hand as she thought. Fred was being a little rude, wandering from one side of the sidewalk to the other until Kenneth would stumble over him. Megan was pretty sure he knew exactly what he was doing. She shortened the leash after the third time.

"Do you have a security system at your house yet?" Kenneth asked, scooting over and giving her and Fred a little more room. He walked comfortably, his long legs and pleasant face somehow matching the upscale neighborhood. "It seems a little unsafe for someone living on their own, is all." He shrugged, his eyes meeting hers briefly. "What do you think?"

"Well." Megan wasn't sure what she thought anymore. Not after meeting with the crazy people at the Dewald Investing Firm. "I suppose you're right, especially with the way Seacrest is growing. It would probably be smart to get one." She eyed him, wondering what had brought that on.

He ran his hand through his hair, looking a little agitated. "I liked that you wore a disguise yesterday, but I noticed you gave them your real name?"

Megan shrugged. "Well, yeah, I had to." She stopped, feeling like they should be headed back, anyway. "If they checked up on my portfolio, I didn't want to give them a fake name."

"I understand," he said, nodding. "That makes sense, but I'm just not sure why they were following you the way they were. It's concerning."

"Yes." She couldn't help laughing a little. "Very concerning. But don't worry." She nudged his arm and turned back toward the house.

He followed, walking in step next to her.

"I've got Fred, and there's really no reason for them to bother me. I think I just should have researched their company a little more. I came off as so completely incompetent that I'm sure they suspected me of digging for information. Probably thought I was a spy from another company or something similar."

"I hope that's all it was." He rubbed the back of his neck, glancing behind them. In fact, now that she thought about it, he glanced around a lot. His gaze was constantly inspecting the houses they passed and the bushes and trees between them.

"Everything all right?" she finally asked as they made it to the gate at his place.

"What?" He paused, giving her a tiny smile. "Oh yeah, fine." He punched in the code and turned around, watching the street to the right and left of them as it opened.

Megan looked around as well before crossing through the entry with Fred. When she reached the steps, she froze, catching sight of a man inside his house.

"Kenneth!" she whispered, alarmed. He hurried to meet up with her. "There's someone in your house."

He glanced in the window and waved a hand in front of them. "It's just my technician working on the power for a few things inside. I've been having trouble with a glitchy connection."

Megan opened the door to see a man closing the box to the security system and pressing a button. He smiled over at them and nodded at Kenneth. "All done, sir."

Kenneth thanked him, and the man left. Megan took a moment to recover from her mini-heart attack, and then she returned to the bedroom to begin packing her things. When she was all finished, she patted the cushy blankets affectionately, tucking the thought away that she just might be able to stay there the next time she came to Seattle.

"I, uh..."

She turned around to see Kenneth in the doorway, wearing a much more customary suit. His hair was smooth and perfect, and he seemed to step into a more professional role, shedding his relaxed self just enough for Megan to miss it.

"Yes?" she asked, pulling the handle on her luggage and wheeling it over to him.

"I have to be heading into the office soon, but I wanted to be sure and see you off first." He hesitated a moment and then turned, heading back to the living area.

Megan followed, wondering again about all the things she could see in his eyes that it seemed he simply refused to say.

Plus, she hated the thought of leaving his house without knowing what was inside the manilla envelope. And yet another part of her mind anticipated her exploration behind Edgewater Estates. What had Santiago hidden there? Treasure? Documents? Still, she gazed down the hall that led to Kenneth's bedroom.

"I'd love to hear from you whenever you feel like giving me a call." Kenneth scooted around so that he was in front of her and he gave her a quick hug. It was nothing like before, when he'd first seen her in his house and had been panicked and glorious. This time, his hug was practically sterile.

Megan stepped out of his embrace with a smile on her lips, determined to remain unaffected from this moment. She and Kenneth were water and air, and imagining any sort of relationship between them was silly. So, she lifted her chin and gave him a playful wink. "Find a new investment company."

A look of surprise crossed his face, but then he laughed, nodding. "Yes," he agreed, "I'll put that on my to-do list, shall I?"

"You shall." Megan pursed her lips as he turned to the front door with a grin across his face. But when she went to leave, he stepped in front of her again. His face had become serious. It was the side of him that she knew only occasionally, the one that made her thoughts swim.

"Be careful, Megan," he said, his voice low. "Just in case."

She had to swallow before answering and remind herself that jumping into his arms would send a conflicting message. In the end, she felt haunted by his dark eyes.

"I will if you will."

He grinned. "Deal."

· · ·

THE TRIP TO HER PARENTS' HOUSE WAS SPENT THINKING OF the last conversation she had with them. They'd supported her move for the first time but hadn't told her about their trip to Hawaii.

Soon enough, she sat in the driveway with her car idling. The home was large, built before it was unreasonably expensive to do so. The natural growth of the trees around it was always something she admired. The way the skinny pines had grown far above the rooftop, and the weeping cherry tree was full and well-established. They matched the house as if painted there.

Fred stared out the window with his tail wagging, looking very interested in this adventure. But she knew her parents would hardly be thrilled to see video footage of a huge canine wandering through their house on their security camera, so she cracked the windows and left him to wait yet again. His eyes were not amused when she got out of the car and glanced back at him.

"I'll get you a treat right after this," she said, although his droopy eyes didn't change. "Promise."

She walked up the steps with memories blazing through her mind. Skipping up the steps coming home from soccer camp, waiting for her dad to get back from work, walking out front to see how the Christmas lights looked. Everything was wonderful. All of it. There were stressful, crazy times and moments of frustration and sadness, but that was okay too. Her parents had shown her what love was and what it could build.

Pushing in the code was as automatic as twisting the handle, and she did both without looking. Her eyes peered in through the decorative glass at the abstract shapes of the interior beyond. She walked in and closed the door behind her. It was calm and clean and smelled good, as always. If her mom didn't have a ginger and cinnamon fragrance plugin somewhere, it wouldn't be home.

Everything seemed to be stunningly in order, from the new coral pillows accented by a beautiful new painting of a field of poppies, to the sparkling appliances. She wandered down the hall and through the bedrooms, double checking that windows were closed and locked and nothing was left turned on or plugged in. She went out the back door and walked a circle around the yard, finding it all as she remembered.

When she entered again, she closed the French doors and locked up again, but something seemed off. She walked down the hall, assuring she'd turned the lights off. Everything was fine. It wasn't until she went to leave that she stumbled to a stop.

Jarron stood just in front of the door, blocking her way. He wasn't smiling, and alarms were going off in Megan's head. If he wasn't trying to work his magic on her, it meant he had other plans.

She took a few slow steps toward him, telling herself that the closer she was to him, the closer she was to the door. And that was her goal. But once she was in front of him, she could see the rosacea in his cheeks and the glassiness to his eyes— the telltale signs that he'd been drinking. She took a slow, steady breath and smelled the scent of alcohol on his breath. The only time she'd ever seen him drunk before had been terrifying. He'd exploded on her, shouting and throwing things. He'd broken a vase he bought for her just the week before. At the time, she'd chalked it up to the lifelong tension between him and his father. But now it was clear as he stood before her practically seething... Jarron and alcohol did not mix well.

Chapter Thirteen

How she wished she'd brought Fred in. They stood at a silent standoff for an uncomfortably long time. Megan took a step to the side as if she would walk around him.

"I'd better be going," she said, hoping his mental state would make him slow to respond. If she could just get out the door so they weren't enclosed together.

"No." He grabbed her arm, marching forward. She rushed back to keep from getting run over, hardly feeling his hand on her arm even though he held her tight. All she could think of was getting away. She wished she'd left the back patio doors open. If she ran, she bet she could make it. But turning the lock and opening the door? Not a chance.

When they were in the middle of the living room, he released her. "I don't understand it," he said, his voice echoing against the vaulted ceilings. "Why, Megan?"

She took a step to the side, hoping to slowly maneuver until he was no longer between her and the door. He didn't budge, remaining rigid in place with only his gaze following her.

"Why what, Jarron?" Her voice was even. Calm. Just keep him calm.

"Why are we not together? Why did you say no? Why won't you marry me?" With each question, his hand flung through the air more violently. She flinched with the last one.

"I said no because we're not right for each other."

"No." He shook his head and a few strands of hair stuck to the sweat on his forehead. "*I'm* not right for *you*." He jabbed a finger back at her. "But you won't tell me *why*."

"Okay," She held a hand up, hoping he would give her time to explain. "You're right, I never told you why. But I'll tell you now." She edged closer to the door as she spoke, one small, gentle step at a time. Ever so carefully.

"I have different dreams than you," She said, speaking softly. "Dreams you don't understand. And that's okay! It's okay to have different dreams. But if we stayed together, one of us would have to give up on our dreams, and that's not fair." She took another slow step, almost ready to run. "Is it?"

He heaved out a gust of air and swayed on his feet, his eyes going out of focus briefly. The phone rang, and he snapped back to attention. "Nah," he said, his words beginning to slur. He glanced at the phone on the kitchen counter. A landline. Not many people had one of those anymore.

If he passed out in her parent's house, what would they think? But then, they'd probably catch all this on their security feed when they got home from their trip. Megan cringed, hoping they wouldn't check it.

Jarron's face hardened and he lunged suddenly. She screamed, dodging his hand that was balled into a fist. He fell to the ground, and Megan dashed for the front door. He caught her foot and she tripped, hitting the tile floor hard on her hands and knees. Flipping over, she kicked, shaking his hand off and sinking the heel of her shoe into his wrist. He didn't react. In fact, he wasn't even moving.

She scrambled to her feet and ran for the door. Wrenching it open, she locked it behind her with shaking hands. Fred barked as she hurried to her car. She could hardly make her fingers work, but after a few agonizing minutes she was in the car. Gripping the steering wheel, she took a deep breath and turned the keys in the ignition backing out quickly.

Whenever Jarron woke up, she wanted to be as far away as possible. She imagined him racing after her, running out the door and ramming her off the road. Her hands continued to shake, but she focused on getting back to Seacrest. On getting home. She'd spent enough time in Seattle.

Fred laid down in his seat but continued staring at her. "It's okay, Fred." She took the on-ramp onto the freeway. "It's okay."

He stretched out until his paw rested on her leg and then closed his eyes. Megan ran one hand across her forehead, hardly able to believe what had just happened. Jarron was stubborn and arrogant, but she'd never felt he was dangerous. Suddenly Seacrest didn't seem far enough away, not if he was still so upset about her saying no after all these months.

She flipped on the radio and settled into the drive, trying to move her thoughts away from Jarron and think about the future. If she wanted to stay in Seacrest, her future would have to include a successful shop, and there was only one business she could think of that wouldn't be too complicated. And that was sandwiches. All she'd need was fresh vegetables and toppings, sauces, meats, and bread. Delicious deli pickles were a must. Buy a few cases of soda and then, *voilà*, she was in business. At least it would be something to bring in an income for a little while.

With her hand over Fred's paw, she stroked his leg. "Sandwiches, Fred." She glanced over to see him twitching in his sleep.

When they pulled up to her house, she had a checklist in her head of all the items she needed. Her old fridge at the shop would have to do for now, and the only equipment she needed was a toaster oven. It would be simple.

She leaned back in her chair with the car still running and closed her eyes, completely wasted. Then again, her adrenaline had been going haywire the last two days. It was no wonder she sank into sleep in a matter of seconds.

In her dream, there were customers crowded around her new sandwich shop. One was dressed in a crab costume and kept pinching her in the rear. Everyone else shouted out their sandwich orders as if they expected them to drop from the sky. Monte Cristo! Grilled cheese! Club sandwich! Turkey Vegetable! Megan placed a hundred slices of bread on the floor and began making sandwiches there because the counter was overloaded with black pearls.

Then Santiago walked in, an old man. He had a gray beard that trailed to the floor and shackles around his wrists and ankles. "Megan," he cried, dragging monstrous chains behind him. "Why didn't you get my sandwich right?"

Megan jolted awake. The plastic water bottle clutched in her hand flew into the back seat.

"What in the world?" she mumbled, rubbing her face. Her backside had fallen asleep, and it tingled painfully. Rubbing one numb cheek, she chuckled at her bizarre dream.

"Let's get outta here, Fred." She turned off the car and popped the hatchback, collecting her things while Fred dashed off into the forest. He looked happy to be back, at least. Her dream had made her wonder if she might need to spend a little more time focusing on herself. Relaxing, perhaps.

She shook her head as she pulled her small suitcase up the steps and into the house. Above the fridge, she could see the corner of the envelope Santiago's lawyer had mailed as if it were welcoming her home.

Remember me? We have a date.

"Just give me a minute," she said, glancing back to see Fred still frolicking in the forest. She closed the door behind her, leaving him to it. It was a strange feeling to be back in Seacrest, especially when she thought back to her foolish plans of imitating a client in order to get some dirt on Santiago's work life. She'd had no idea what she was doing, that much was clear.

Still, she'd gotten a taste of just how passionate Lyanna was about finding the black pearl necklace. How shockingly serious the matter was. In fact, she'd call it borderline insanity. But Santiago knew Megan had a necklace like the one from the legend. Why hadn't he just asked her about it? She walked to her bathroom, remembering Lyanna's condition of finding the necklace before she would marry. It sounded very close to a threat against her poor fiancé.

She pulled open a small side drawer, and lifted the necklace out as chills tingled down her back. It was beautiful, yes. But centuries old and belonging to Cleopatra? She let the light shine across each smoldering, inky black orb.

There was no way.

But just in case... she took it to the side table next to her bed and tucked it underneath, out of sight. It was perhaps a better hiding place than her bathroom drawer, but not by much. She'd have to rent out a safety deposit box at the local bank soon. But for now, it would be getting dark, and all she'd had to eat was snack food on the drive. She returned to the kitchen and started a pot of water on the stove and pulled out a bag of pasta.

Slicing vegetables and stirring a skillet of simmering red sauce, it was an easy meal. But as she sat down to eat, she appreciated the warm home-cooked goodness after a couple of days on the road. It warmed her body and soul and left her feeling more comfortable in her home. The memory of standing in front of Jarron at his high-rise apartment condo flashed through her mind. In his hand, he'd held a ridiculously oversized ring. It was exactly the type of jewelry she never wore, but he didn't realize it. Of course. He'd never spent much time getting to know her. Rather, he seemed pleased at how well she complimented him.

She'd always thought things would get better. If they could just take some time off together or go to the coast or on a hike... but somehow their days were constantly planned away. Jarron had their schedules hopping from one celebrity event to the next. At least, when he wasn't tied up in golf tournaments. It was someone's dream, to be sure. Just not hers.

She sighed, running a hand through her hair and gazing across her house. The sun had set, leaving a soft glowing sky behind. It was still light, but it would fade quickly now. The forest was beautiful this time of night, and the glow of the sky reflected in the ocean, creating a seamless transition between them. Seacrest was a dream worth working on. And now, with no one but herself to answer to, there was a surprisingly small amount of guilt in her life.

Fred scratched at the door, and she went to let him in. His nose told a story of dirt and digging before he'd even stepped foot inside.

"Fred," she grumbled. But she was too tired for bath time, so she settled with soaking a few rags in warm, soapy water and giving him a sponge bath. He stood still and allowed it, as if he were tired as well and agreed that bath time would be far too much work. The next day she could go hiking behind Edgewater Estates like Santiago's message said. Even if she had a feeling he'd turned his attention to Kenneth.

"Not a chance," she mumbled, after she was showered and

dressed in her cozy cotton pajamas. Her head sank into her pillow, and her eyes closed. "I'll get there first."

Fred jumped up, curling himself onto the end of her bed so that his body was warm and heavy on her toes. It was the first time he'd ever opted to sleep anywhere other than the rug by the fireplace. She glanced down at him, considering telling him to get down. But then, her toes had never been so warm, and even amidst her deliberations, she fell asleep.

Chapter Fourteen

Megan's phone rang when the house was still dark. She glanced at the time on her screen. It was barely 5 a.m. She answered with a groggy *hello*.

"Meg!"

Her mother's voice blasted in her ear, and she moved the phone away in reaction. "What is it, Mom?"

Her heart was pounding, but somehow, she was more annoyed than scared. Clearly, if her parents were calling her at 5 a.m., that meant it probably wasn't a *real* emergency, but simply a *minor* emergency. And a minor emergency could at least wait until 7 a.m. Now that she was up, it would be impossible to get back to sleep, and she would be a zombie the entire day. Fred heaved a big breath from his spot at her feet, agreeing.

"Hun, are you okay?" her mom asked.

"We called the police," her father's voice chimed in from the background.

"What?" Megan sat up, refusing to switch on the light. Maybe there was still a small chance her brain wasn't overly stimulated yet, and she could get back to bed. But with the way her curiosity neurons were firing, she doubted it.

"We saw what Jarron did." Her father's voice came again, louder this time. "We reported it and turned the recording into the police. I'm sure he's in jail now or at least being questioned."

Megan's face suddenly felt numb. Sure, Jarron made a stupid decision by threatening her, but didn't arresting him mean she would have to come make a statement, at least? Acid churned in her stomach at the thought. Would he be watching when she made the statement?

She bit her lip. "Will I need to come out again?"

"We gave them your information, so they'll be getting ahold of you, dear." Her mom had taken over again. "We just needed to call and say we're so sorry. If he was treating you like this, why didn't you ever say anything?"

"He wasn't treating me like that. I mean, once he got angry when he'd had a lot to drink. But he isn't much of a drinker, so it wasn't something I ever saw again. Until yesterday." She rubbed her eyes. "Could we talk about this later? I'm still pretty tired from my trip."

"Absolutely, hun." Her mom's voice was filled with the compassion of a worried parent.

"Give us a call later, then," her dad said. "Bye, Megan."

"Bye Mom, bye Dad."

She ended the call and dropped her phone to the rug, covering herself in blankets. It was eerie to realize Jarron was sitting in jail at that moment. Even though she knew it was him who'd crossed the line, she couldn't help feeling bad about it. Strange the things people would resort to when they were desperate. Her thoughts slowly wandered back to the necklace under her nightstand. Lyanna couldn't possibly know about it, but the question of what she would do if she did never seemed to leave. Megan could imagine a great many unpleasant possibilities.

After going over the conversation with her parents a hundred times in her head, she relented to the fact that she wasn't going to fall asleep again. Fred groaned and lifted from his comfortable position. His sleep had clearly been ruined as well. He stepped down from the bed, which was easy with his long legs, and walked to the other room. She could hear him lapping from his water bowl along with the sloppy splashes of water on the floor. He was a messy drinker.

She slid out of bed and walked into the kitchen. Standing on her toes, she pulled the envelope from the top of the fridge. It had been too many days since Santiago had asked her to come to Seattle. Too many days since he'd spoken to her in code, asking her to do something he considered dangerous. But at the moment, no news was focused on Seacrest. If that changed, it would be very hard for her to follow his instructions without anyone noticing.

With a heavy breath, she replaced the envelope. She didn't need it anyway; she'd already memorized the instructions. After feeding Fred and eating a quick bowl of cereal, she got dressed in an old pair of jeans and a dark sweatshirt. The day looked like it might rain, and she wanted to be ready. Besides, dark colors would stand out less. She loaded a day pack with a granola bar, apple, and water, along with a flashlight and first aid kit. If she had any climbing gear, she would have thrown it in, but as it was, she just crossed her fingers that the note was perhaps misleading, and she wouldn't be scaling a cliff-face.

"You ready?" she asked Fred, walking out to the patio and taking her bike down the steps. It seemed a less conspicuous way to go about things, as her little hatchback was the only one she'd ever seen in the area. If someone spotted it, they would have no trouble figuring out who it belonged to. Her

Great Dane was also pretty signaling, but she ignored that fact.

With a steadying breath, she headed down the forest trail that wound through the woods and behind the boardwalk. Though it hadn't rained, the ground was wet with fog and dew from the night before. It was quiet in the early morning, even for a weekday. Shops had yet to open, and the only life she saw was lined up at the coffee truck. She took another trail uphill that led to the back of the Estates. Fred trotted along beside her, but his behavior was different. Instead of becoming distracted by every song bird and chittering squirrel, he was oddly focused, as if he knew there was a task ahead.

At the back of the upscale neighborhood, there was a sandy trail nearly covered in dune grass. She followed it cautiously, wishing he'd given her more of a direction than just *behind the Estates*. That could be anywhere along the cliffs. How would she ever find a rope?

The trail led closer and closer to the edge of the cliff where gusts of wind were beginning to blow up and over the edge of the land, coming off the sea. It was unnerving to hear the shuttering of dune grasses around her and then have it silenced as the wind subsided. Gust after gust rushed by, and slowly she got a little more used to the rhythm. It wasn't strong enough to shake much more than her confidence, so she kept going. She reached the curve of the trail that came closest to the edge, where grasses gave way to rock, and settled her bike against a boulder. She released Fred's leash, letting him explore while she searched. He dropped his nose to the earth and began following scent trails.

The ocean was much farther down than she'd realized, but then she'd never come so close to the edge. It fanned out in a glorious view, especially with the sunrise coming on. She didn't dare lean over the cliff's edge to look below. Instead, she walked a crisscrossing path along the rocky ground, looking for any clue that there might be a way down to the beach. To her surprise, it didn't take long to find what she was looking for.

A rope was tied around a skinny, pointy rock that jutted upward from a cluster of stones. It was a strange part of the landscape, where the rocks were so tightly wedged together, it was difficult to see anything beyond. If anyone were to come that way, they would naturally veer to one side or the other, to view the coastline again.

She crept closer, only to have Fred barrel past, bumping into her. Stumbling to the side, she watched him stop at the rope and begin sniffing furiously, keenly interested in the rock and a section between the boulder next to it. There was a small area where she could possibly squeeze between the two, and that was where Fred sniffed. His tail whipped back and forth, and he paced a small circle only to return to that very spot again.

When she reached the first rock, she settled her palm against it, relieved to feel it sturdy and unmoving. As solid as a mountain. She patted around her, pushing each boulder, satisfied when they were all wedged into place as if they'd stood for ages. And they likely had. It was the Estates that were new, not the cliffs.

The rope looked heavy and unworn, although it was clear it had been used before. It was a pale tan and green color, blending with the surroundings well. If she hadn't been looking for it, she never would have spotted it. A figure eight climber's knot was double tied, and she scooted her feet forward slowly, pulling at the end that dangled off the cliff. It moved a little, rubbing against the rocks. She edged along a little farther, making her way between the rocks. Glancing back, she saw Fred had sat at some point, and his head was tilted as he watched her.

She took a careful breath, holding her hand up. "Stay, Fred," she cautioned, turning back to the rocks. They stretched out farther than she'd thought before the view dropped off. Her hands became sweaty just thinking about looking over the edge. She managed a few more steps, while still clinging to the rope, and then she saw it. The rope she held in her hand led right to a rope ladder. The top was just visible, bolted into the rock the way climbers might secure an anchor.

Lowering to her knees, she crawled the remaining distance and laid on her belly. There was a carabiner clipped to the top of the ladder. She lifted it up to find a harness attached, secured to the ladder. Scooting forward a little more, she looked off the edge of the cliff.

There were handles anchored into the rock on each side of the ladder and the ladder itself was secured down. It wasn't a straight plummet to the ground, like she'd imagined. Instead, the cliff face was rounded, giving it a gentler decent. It might even be more like crawling down a hill than scaling a cliff. At least, that was what she told herself. But her sweaty hands were arguing with her. She turned back toward Fred, but the rocks obscured any sight of him.

She reached for the harness and adjusted her position until she was sitting. Her legs slid easily into the straps, and she tightened it at her waist. Taking the rope in her hand again, she repeated Santiago's message in her head as she placed her feet on the first rung. It was strong and wide, like a heavy strip of canvas. She placed all her weight on it and reached for the next with her toe. One step after the other, she lowered. Carefully and cautiously. The wind didn't bother her anymore. In fact, there was hardly any fear left in her. Once she'd strapped the harness on and felt the security of the ladder, she was excited to keep going. Every step, she told herself she could go back if she wanted, but she continued on.

The round part of the cliff straightened out, and she looked down to see the ladder hanging straight down through the air until it ended on the sand below. It wasn't far, maybe twenty feet. She held on tight and took one step after the other. When her feet settled onto the beach, she sighed with relief and loosened the harness, stepping out of it.

She'd made it. But now, she had to figure out what it was Santiago wanted her to find. She knew now why he said she would be in danger, but why would he send her to an isolated beach accessed only by rope ladder? She began walking, but the cliff jutted out into the ocean on one side, hedging her way any farther. Still, she continued on until she'd reached it. Portions of the rock were wet, as if the water rose often. She turned and walked toward the other end. It looked like the cliff would block her path in that direction too, but there was a good stretch of beach to cover.

It wasn't until she'd passed it that she realized what was there. A cave in the side of the cliff. It was full of water like a small lake, with a stream issuing from it and spilling out across the sand, emptying out into the ocean. A pool likely filled at high tide and left isolated at low, which meant she wouldn't want to be there for too long. She didn't know how much time she had until high tide. It didn't look like it would be soon, as there was still a good-sized beach between the cave and the ocean. But the one thing she could depend on when it came to the ocean, was how undependable it was. Plus, Fred might begin to wander the longer she made him wait.

She walked inside, and her eyes adjusted to the darkness to reveal a yacht at the far end of the cave, floating in the huge pool of seawater. Mystified, she walked along the edge, where the sand was piled up and dry, and circled to the back wall. The yacht was anchored and had a makeshift dock of wood pallets tied together. She made her way across the wobbly structure and climbed up onto the deck. It was a beautiful boat, but it felt eerie in the absolute silence of the cave. She continued below deck, switching on lights as she went.

There was a comfortable cabin that opened up into a living area with a couch and a small coffee table. She walked forward slowly and settled down on the couch. Because there, in front of her on the table, was a laptop. After a deep breath, she placed her hands on the keys. Typing in Santiago's name, she pressed enter. But the password bar bounced right and left, telling her no. She tried again, this time typing in his last name as well. Still no.

Her gaze wandered and suddenly she remembered the key word he'd given her to break the code. If he was a genius, he just might have been giving her much more than that. She typed it into the password bar slowly. T-R-E-S.

The screen melted away to a desktop. One icon had been saved to the screen. A scorpion. She slid the cursor over it and clicked. Instantly, audio began to play. Santiago's voice blared from his computer. Her heart raced at hearing him ask, *what do you want?* There was no answer.

His voice came again.

"Maybe I could trust you if you'd turn off your voice altering software. Why can't I know who you are? How am I supposed to take your advice if you're hiding your identity from me?"

Another pause. Megan assumed it was a phone recording, which was why the other person wasn't recorded.

Santiago's voice continued, *"I know what's going on, and if I report it to police, they'll find out who you are. You need to leave my company alone."*

There was a long stretch of silence. Megan glanced down to see there was still two minutes left on the recording. She waited.

"What do my parents have to do with this?"

The question was uttered in low, threatening tones.

"There are many similar necklaces. Ms. Henny's is a fake."

She started at hearing her name, straining to catch the rest. But there was no more, only a sigh before the recording cut out. The icon flickered and disappeared from the desktop.

Something shifted behind her, and there was a small creak in the floor. Her gaze shot up from the screen. She spun around, but it was too late. A cloth pressed against her face with a scent that stung her nose and burned in her lungs. She tried to cry out, but the darkness came too swiftly.

Chapter Fifteen

When Megan awoke, the room was dark, and her head was splitting with pain. She turned slowly, lifting from where she was collapsed on the couch.

The laptop was gone.

She sat up too quickly, and a rush of nausea followed. Breathing through it, she took a moment before trying to stand. There was still a light on in the cabin, and up the stairs to the deck above, it reflected light from outside. So, at least she knew it was still daylight. Her mind was so mixed up, she worried a whole day might have passed. Stumbling forward, she pulled her phone from her pocket to see it was past two in the afternoon. But there was no signal, at least not in the cave.

She navigated the pallet dock with an unsteady step, but managed to make it to the sandy edge. Rushing around, she was finally out of the cave. Her phone had a small signal, and she typed in Crystal's number. At the rope ladder, the harness hung at the end. So, the mysterious person had likely climbed up with nothing.

"Hi, Megan," Crystal answered with a cheerful voice, and Megan imagined her bent over her craft table, making intricate jewelry.

Megan threaded her legs through the harness and tightened it around her waist. "Hey, I'm in a bit of trouble," she said. "I don't feel completely safe taking my bike home right now. I'm at the Estates. Is there any way you could give me a ride?" She held the rope, waiting until she could put her phone back in her pocket to climb.

"Absolutely," Crystal said quickly. "Let me just lock up the shop. No one's here right now anyway, so it's fine. I'll head over there in two minutes. Okay?"

"Thank you so much," Megan's head continued to throb, but she pushed the pain to the back of her mind as much as she could and tucked her phone away, beginning up the rope. It seemed much more difficult than the way down had, especially when the throbbing in her head grew worse. She swallowed hard, focusing on the next rung up, and the next. Until finally, she made it to the top.

She crawled up onto the edge of the cliff, searching for Fred. She called his name, but there was no answer. Wind billowed from the ocean, leaving her dangerously off balance. She crawled forward before getting to her feet and running back to her bike. It was still leaning against the rock where she left it. She began to walk it back through the Estates, coming out behind one of the houses and onto the sidewalk.

There wasn't anyone outside in the windy afternoon, which made it that much easier to see Crystal's comfortable sedan come up the hill. She stopped right in front of Megan and the trunk popped open. Crystal hopped out of the car.

"Can I help you with that?" she asked. Her eyes lingered on Megan's face. "Are you feeling okay? Your face is pale."

"No, it's fine. Thank you." Megan hurried to lift her bike

in and then got in the front. Once Crystal was in, she nodded her head down the road. "I'm just worried about Fred. He was here waiting for me, but I think he ran home before I got back."

Crystal had begun driving, but she glanced back at Megan. "He was waiting for you to do what, exactly?"

Megan's head continued to throb, but she tried to think of any reason why she'd be hiking around behind the Estates. "Uh..." She scanned the area around them, still searching for Fred. What if the person who'd attacked her had also gotten to Fred? "I..." Nothing was coming to her, so she only glanced back at Crystal. Her friend was looking worried.

"You can tell me, Megan." Her eyes had widened, and she looked truly afraid.

"I'm sorry, Crystal." Megan sighed, swallowing again as another surge of pain filled her head. She closed her eyes and lifted one cold hand to the clammy skin of her forehead. "I really don't feel well, but I'm not sick. I just..." She sighed. "I followed these crazy instructions Santiago gave me and ended up taking a rope ladder down the cliffs behind the Estates. It led to a cave, and inside, it was a yacht I can only assume is his. There was a laptop inside with a recording."

She shook her head, opening her eyes to see Crystal's lips were parted. Her friend stared down the road silently with widened eyes.

"Anyway," Megan continued, watching her. "Someone came up behind me when I was listening to it, and they covered my face with something." Her head pounded, and she rubbed her hand across her forehead again. "I was out for a few hours, and I just now climbed back up."

"Oh my goodness, Megan." Crystal had already driven past the boardwalk and was on the street leading to Megan's house. But she pressed on the brakes suddenly, bringing them to a stop in the middle of the road. "I can't just take you back to your house. What if they went there next? We need to go to the police station."

Megan shook her head. "I can't. I'd have to tell them about the yacht, and then they'd go search it. I mean, clearly he doesn't want anyone to know it's there."

"Well." Crystal shrugged. "How do you know we're safe out here?"

Megan thought it over, still focused on the chilling possibility that Fred had been caught up in the middle of everything. What if he wasn't at home? What if she never saw him again? She took a sudden breath. "Let's just go to the house and see if Fred is there. If anything feels off, we'll leave."

Crystal hesitated a moment, and after a long look at Megan, she finally agreed. Her foot eased off the brakes. "Okay, but we're staying in the car."

"Deal," Megan said.

They approached Megan's house, and when it came into view, there was a car parked next to it. Megan's breath caught in her throat until she recognized the sleek silver vehicle. She nodded encouragingly to Crystal. "It's Kenneth," she said, stepping out of the car the moment they stopped.

She walked slowly, hoping Fred would come around the corner. But instead, Kenneth appeared on the deck. His face was flushed and his eyes wide. He jogged down the steps and pulled her into his arms.

"Megan," he gasped. "Oh my gosh. I thought..." His words faded away, and he held her tightly.

"Kenneth?" Megan's heart was pounding against him. It was so confusing, as if he knew everything that had just happened. She needed to explain, but instead found herself clinging to him and struggling to breathe through a wave of fear.

His arms began to release her, and with one last deep breath, she let go. His eyes were afraid, but as events came into focus, she realized he couldn't possibly know what had just happened in the cave. His worried eyes looked past her to Crystal. Megan turned to see her friend approaching them cautiously, with the same confusion on her face.

"Okay, you two." Kenneth's hands had lingered on Megan's arms, but they dropped as his look of suspicion deepened. "Where have you been?"

Megan met Crystal's eyes and then swallowed, turning to Kenneth. "Why?"

His eyebrow lifted, likely in reaction to the way she'd neglected to answer. Then he nodded back at them and reached into his jacket, pulling out the manilla envelope. It was folded in half, and he opened it, smoothing out the crease as he spoke.

"Santiago was afraid to turn to you again since he'd learned who was swapping out the authentic pieces of jewelry and trading them for fakes."

Kenneth shook his head, running his hand through his black hair. It had grown considerably longer since they'd first met, sweeping across his gaze when it got the chance. "I'm so sorry, Megan. I should have been more forthcoming with you."

Megan squinted back at him. "What do you mean?"

"Back at my place, after you left your secret agent interview." His lips pressed together in a tight grin, and then it faded away. His gaze solemnified. "I called my security company to tighten up my home security system. It seemed to me that you were in more danger than either of us suspected. And then, when I read these..."

He handed the envelope to Megan, and she took it in her hands, looking down at his name and address on the front.

"I wanted security tightened here as well," Kenneth said. He looked back at her house. "I should have just talked to you about it, but I didn't think I could fully explain without telling you the things Santiago had asked me to handle alone. I thought maybe I could just install it first and then, I don't know, ask your forgiveness." He uttered a dry laugh, but his expression was pained.

Something wasn't making sense, and Megan folded her arms around the envelope, peering back at him. "And this is why you were so worried about me just now?"

He hesitated to answer, his eyes wandering as if searching out what to say. Instead, he placed his arm across her shoulders and turned to the deck. "C'mon, I'll show you."

Megan imagined a great many things as they approached her front door, one of them being that Fred was badly hurt... or worse. She was shaking so hard when she reached for the handle and pushed the door open, she was sure Kenneth could feel it. But what she saw had her gasping.

She took a few quick steps into her house and then stopped, gazing around in shock. It was ransacked. The couch overturned, the rug mangled, every kitchen cabinet opened with their contents piled onto the floor. She rushed to her bedroom, stepping over a fallen lamp and a pile of books strewn from her bookcase. Her bedroom was the same, as was the bathroom. Her blankets and mattress were flung about, her clothes pulled from her dresser and left in heaps on the floor.

She knelt down slowly and swept her hand under her nightstand. Her hand slid across only carpet; it was just as she feared. The necklace was gone. With a hard swallow, she stood again, catching something else among the clutter. She followed a trail of muddy paw prints through the house, stopping in front of Kenneth and Crystal in the living room. She bent down and wiped at a patch of mud, looking up at Kenneth. "Have you seen Fred?"

He shook his head gently. "I haven't."

Megan sat down on the floor next to the trail of muddy prints and opened the envelope. There were three pages inside, and she slid them out, flipping through them. Kenneth sat down on the floor next to her, as did Crystal. They watched her silently as she flipped past the photograph of the lawyer's assistant, Derek, and selected the note from Santiago. She began reading slowly, trying to focus on the words and not on the panic of losing Fred.

Santiago's voice rang out in her mind as she read, explaining that he'd known Derek a few years earlier. They'd attended the same college for a time and had gotten acquainted through a club where students worked together to learn coding and how to develop web applications. They built a quick friendship.

But when he was arrested, and Derek appeared as the associate for his lawyer, Santiago was immediately suspicious. The coincidence was just too strong. So, he dug into the life of his former friend as much as he could. He learned that Derek had spent considerable time in both France and Switzerland, the two countries where Santiago handled the sales and distribution of jewelry for his family's business, Fitch Inc.

Next, Santiago spoke of being afraid for her safety. He worried that by asking her to come out, he'd exposed her to a very dangerous man. His fears led to Derek being fired and Mr. Yost immediately beginning a very secret investigation against him.

He mentioned being commissioned to find a fabled black pearl necklace and admitted he'd thought of Megan's string of pearls, but that he was very scientific in how he researched missing items.

"*Shiny distractions are just that, and anyone who makes a profession out of finding lost items knows you can't just chase hunches. It takes research and knowing your history, so I started there. But I admit, I was afraid someone else might suspect her jewelry as being the one.*"

But it was the end of the letter that had Megan tearing up.

"*Please,*" Santiago's hand-penned words said, "*Take incredible care of Megan. I'm so afraid that my thoughtless actions have put her in danger. I trust you to keep her safe, and I know you have the means of accomplishing this. Please, Kenneth.*" There was no goodbye, no signature. Just those two words left ringing in her ears.

Please, Kenneth.

She flipped through to the final page, glancing over it to see a legal timeline of Santiago's court dates. He only had a handful of days to be cleared before his hearing on Monday. Lowering the papers, she looked back at Kenneth's gentle smile. It was downturned at the edges, as if he still laid the blame on himself. With a sigh, she looked back at Crystal.

Her friend had stayed silent through it all, but now her eyes bored into Megan's. "You should tell him what happened," she said, tipping her head ever so slightly to Kenneth. The look of trust on her face was endearing, especially now that Megan knew their history together. If Kenneth had been dishonest to her once, it was clear that things had changed since then.

Megan's hands were shaking again, or maybe they'd never stopped. Her head continued to throb, but thankfully, it had dulled somewhat. It left her mind clear enough to recall everything that had happened, and she told Kenneth about it as she returned the papers to their place in the manilla envelope. She didn't want to see the concern in his eyes when she mentioned the cloth pressed to her face, so she stared down at her hands instead, studying them until she was finished.

Silence hovered around them, giving her time to process everything she'd gotten herself into. Gazing across her house again, and all the destruction, she knew there was no choice. She had to go to the police.

Kenneth stood, taking her arms gently. "Here," he said, helping her to her feet. "Does your head hurt?"

"It's not as bad as it was," Megan said, but standing so suddenly had created another wave of throbbing and nausea. She closed her eyes and breathed deeply.

"Crystal, can you?" Kenneth asked. Crystal wrapped her arm around Megan quickly while Kenneth lifted the couch on its feet again and replaced the cushions.

He nodded and Crystal helped Megan forward until she'd sat down. It felt like they were overreacting, and Megan wanted to object, but sinking into the cushions was such a relief that she couldn't. She lay on the pillow Kenneth brought and closed her eyes when he draped a knitted throw over her.

"Thank you," Megan said quietly. "I'm sure I'll feel better in just a few minutes."

Her eyes closed, and she listened to them talking softly in the kitchen. She just needed a little rest, and then she was going to get started on everything. Calling the police, searching for Fred, cleaning her house. It really wouldn't take that long once she had her energy back. Her heart throbbed when she thought of Fred, and she wanted so badly to feel better, to jump up and call for him. But for the moment, she had no choice. All she could do was allow time to pass and the effects of the mysterious chemical to clear. Then she could look for him.

He would be fine; she was sure. He had to be. The necklace had undoubtedly been found, and so the mysterious person had no reason to go after Fred. Surely he'd run off when they began destroying the place, and he would return home when he felt safe. All she had to do was be patient. Fred would be fine. She repeated that phrase again and again as sleep drew closer.

He'll be fine.

Chapter Sixteen

A gentle hand shook her shoulder lightly.

"Megan," Kenneth whispered. Her eyes opened to see him kneeling in front of her, holding her phone in his hand. "It's your parents." He brushed a few strands of hair out of her face, tucking them behind her ear. "Do you want me to tell them you'll call back? They sounded a little worried, so I wasn't sure."

"No, I'll take it." Megan pushed off the couch, rising slowly to a sitting position. Kenneth's hands were on her arms as if ready for her to collapse.

"Are you sure?" he asked, looking like he regretted waking her.

She combed one hand through her hair and realized, with great relief, that her head had stopped aching. "I'm sure," she said, smiling back at him.

He handed her phone over.

"Thank you," she said, touching his arm and looking into his eyes, hoping to relay the appropriate measure of her gratitude. He tipped his head with a soft smile on his lips and returned to the kitchen, leaving her to her conversation.

"Hey, dear." Her mother's greeting was cautious, and Megan could have guessed, word for word, the question that came next. "And who was that?"

She smiled, glancing back to see Crystal sipping at a mug with steam rising from the rim, and Kenneth with his back to her. He was looking out the front window with his arms folded as if deep in thought. "Just a friend of mine." She watched him turn around and couldn't help throwing him a quick wink. He looked like he rather enjoyed it, and a smile spread across his face. He had a very handsome smile. But her mother's next words had her thoughts scattering.

"You need to come to Seattle and make a statement, dear."

"What?" Megan turned around, sinking into the couch and crossing her legs under her. "Why?"

"Well, quite frankly, because you were the only one there. We have the video footage, but it's difficult to see your lips, and Jarron's back is to the camera."

Megan groaned. It was the last thing in the world she wanted to do. Besides, he was impaired at the time and passed out the moment he'd made a move at her. Couldn't they just let it go? She thought of telling her mother this, but again, she already knew what the answer would be. Her parents had trusted Jarron, and when they went after an injustice, they went hard.

"Okay," She sighed, "I will, but I have a lot going on right now. I don't know when I could come out to Seattle."

"Actually, now that I think about it, I believe they can do it on video," her mother said. "But either way, they'll be getting hold of you."

"Oh, I see." Megan relaxed a little, now that she didn't have to go driving back to Seattle. Fred would no doubt hate the drive as well. She sat up straighter, anxious about Fred again, and looking around the house with new eyes. Suddenly, she noticed that practically everything had been straightened. The kitchen was back in order, and the living room was picked up. From what she could see of her bedroom, it had been cleaned as well.

The paw prints had also been wiped from the floor.

"Megan?"

She focused again on the phone pressed to her ear, realizing it wasn't the first time her mother had said her name. "Yes," she rushed, "Sorry, Mom. I'm doing great. I just have a lot to catch up on, and my house still needs a lot of work as well."

"I understand." Her mother wasn't one to draw things out, which she was very grateful for. "Keep me informed on your statement. I can help in any way you'd like, and your dad and I can come out to Seacrest for a while if you need? Your father loves odd projects around the house, and I've started up a business before. We're here for you. Don't forget that, okay?"

They were the words she'd been hoping to hear from day one, only it had taken her parents finally seeing Jarron's dark side for her to hear them. In a strange way, she was grateful for that. "Thanks, Mom," she said quietly, "I really appreciate it."

They said their goodbyes and Megan stood from the couch, feeling a thousand times better than she had when she'd lain down. The afternoon was late, with evening on its heels.

"Any sign of Fred?" she asked, joining Crystal and Kenneth in the kitchen. They both looked back at her for a silent moment before anyone answered. Megan opened the back door, peering into the forest.

"Nothing yet," Kenneth said from behind her.

"I'm sure he'll be back soon," Crystal chimed in. She

joined Megan and scanned the trees with her. "Doesn't he explore the woods often?"

"Yes." Megan sighed. "But..." She walked out onto the deck, leaning against the railing. "I'm just worried about him. He was at the cliffs, and obviously, he came back. But what happened after that?"

Crystal walked to the end of the deck and frowned at the forest. "I don't know," she said quietly.

"Megan."

They both turned around to see Kenneth in the doorway. He'd put his coat on, and he closed the door behind him. "I've called a security company, if you're okay with that? My gift to you, really. I'd never get any sleep if you didn't have it. They'll be here early tomorrow morning." He looked down at the deck, shifting his weight from one foot to the other.

"I'd feel so much better if you could stay with myself or Crystal tonight." His stormy eyes lifted to meet hers, and Megan's heart tightened in her chest.

"I don't know," she managed to say, even though she did know. She would be happy to stay with Kenneth, but then... maybe it wasn't the best idea to rush off with him when she was already feeling so shaky inside. She was afraid for Fred and terrified of who might have attacked her. It left her practically desperate for comfort.

"I do have an incredible security system," Crystal said. She had an easy smile on her face and shrugged a customary lift of her shoulders. "I'd be happy to have you."

Megan's cheeks flushed as she thought about turning back to Kenneth. For some reason, she couldn't bear the thought of looking into his eyes again. She focused on Crystal, fighting the urge to see his face. "I'd love that, thank you," she finally managed. "I'll just go pack a bag, and we can head over now. Fred knows his way around town. We might find him on the drive over."

"I took some pictures and sent them to the police chief," Kenneth said. "He wanted to meet with you tomorrow afternoon. If, uh..." He hesitated when Megan's eyes finally shifted to him, as if it caught him off guard.

She tried to hide the turmoil inside, but felt it radiating from her face in mighty waves.

"If that's all right with you?" Kenneth asked. His voice had quieted, and he took a small step forward as if it couldn't be helped.

"That's probably better, anyway," Crystal said, seeming oblivious to the tension between them. They each straightened a bit in reaction to her matter-of-fact voice.

"I'll just go..." She looked from Kenneth to Megan and back again, as if she'd noticed something was off. "I'll just wait in the car." With that, she smiled tersely and strode down the steps of the deck, rounding the corner of the house. Her car engine revved to life and echoed slightly through the quiet treetops.

Megan hadn't looked away from Kenneth even to respond to Crystal. She felt like she was sinking in his gaze, wishing only to thank him for everything. And yet, her voice was lost.

He took a slow step closer, appearing caught in the same battle as Megan. She could see it in his eyes, the struggle to understand what was between them. But with another step, his hand lifted. It settled gently on her cheek and trailed down until his fingers were just under her chin. His other hand touched her back, and she moved effortlessly closer to him. He bent at the waist, tilting her head upward ever so slightly.

Megan was caught in his gaze, his closeness leaving her breathless. She reached for him, one hand on his chest and the other atop the hand that held her face. He kissed her gently, moving slowly as if he were dizzy as well. She could barely feel her feet on the deck or her body at all. There was only the spinning of her head and the fire on her lips.

His phone rang, and the melody jolted through the silence. Kenneth jerked back, his breath in her face. He ignored his phone. Megan fought to catch her breath as well, feeling completely unsure of this moment and wanting more at the same time. There were too many emotions battling inside; she knew that. Fears and unknowns, so many that she'd reached for him as if he were her last breath. She knew the reasons, and she knew the dangers. But it didn't stop her from pushing up to her toes and kissing him again.

This time she was more in control, and a smile spread across his lips as he kissed her back. When they separated, he pulled her into a hug, and she could feel his heart pounding.

"I don't know what just happened," he whispered. "If you're feeling afraid, I... I don't want to take advantage of that."

Megan bit her lip, wanting to object, but knowing in her core that he was right. She *was* afraid, and her fear had tangled her up inside. Even knowing that, she couldn't deny the attraction between them. It was worth holding on to... and so she did. She stepped a little closer, lifting on her toes and wrapping both arms around his neck with a sigh.

His arms settled more comfortably around her, and his heart continued to race. She could feel it beating away, betraying his struggles. She slid one hand up his back, combing her fingers through his hair. He leaned away, and she knew he was going to kiss her again.

A car door closed, and there was the sound of footsteps on the gravel. They were frozen, tangled together and looking into each other's eyes longingly. But as a foot struck the step of the deck, Kenneth released her, moving back and turning to the woods with both his hands on the railing.

Megan felt faint, standing there with empty arms. Before

Crystal could come around the corner of the deck, she fled. Racing inside, she hurried to the bedroom and pulled her duffel bag from the closet, shoving her clothes inside. Her eyes were unfocused, and her mind only replayed their kiss over and over again in her head. Finally, she sat on her heels and took a deep breath, running both hands over her face. Her whole frame was shaking, and suddenly she wanted to cry. It burst into her lungs and throbbed painfully, filling her eyes with tears.

She pressed one hand to her chest, working to calm the devastating emotions. She wiped at the tears that escaped and slowed her breathing, hoping to ease any redness in her face. The front door opened and footsteps followed. Brushing at her cheeks, she opened the bottom drawer in her dresser and selected a pair of pajamas, shoving them in her bag. It was the last thing she needed, and with one final breath, she stood, facing Crystal.

Her friend stood at the entry to her bedroom and her eyes widened. "Are you crying?" she asked, her voice booming through the quiet house. Megan could only hope Kenneth was out of earshot as she attempted an explanation.

"It's just too much," she said, feeling the truth of that statement clear to her bones. "I'm afraid for me, for Fred, for Santiago. It's so hard to take."

And that was it. The truth as to why she'd clung to Kenneth like a lifeline in the middle of the ocean. The way she'd desperately wanted him to take her away from reality. And there there was the gut-wrenching realization that it would have been a horrible mistake. They were nowhere near a serious relationship, having only shared one timid kiss and a few glances until today. And now, she worried she might have just ruined a very good thing.

Her friend's gaze was piercing and intelligent, keenly

searching out her face. "Are you sure that's all it is?" she asked quietly.

Megan couldn't deny it. Somehow, Crystal knew. Maybe she'd spoken with Kenneth before she'd come in the house, or she'd seen him storming away. Whatever it was, she knew the tears on Megan's face were more than just fear. Megan's lip shook as she looked deep into Crystal's eyes, and she struggled with her next breath.

"I don't know," she finally admitted, with tears blurring her vision yet again.

Crystal didn't need anything more. She simply wrapped Megan in a tight squeeze and took the bag from her hands. "C'mon, let's go."

Megan blinked away her tears and took a steady breath, following Crystal out onto the deck. She scanned the forest one last time. "But what if Fred comes back?"

"Does he have a food bowl?" Crystal asked. "We could leave some food and a blanket out on the deck in case he comes back before you do."

"Good idea." Megan hurried back. She grabbed her thickest flannel throw from beside the fireplace and folded it, laying it on the deck. The food bowl she filled with kibble and placed next to it before turning to the forest again.

She called his name three times, waiting after each attempt and listening for any response. But the forest was still, no rustling leaves, no barking. If he were anywhere nearby and able to respond, he would have.

Crystal waited by the steps of the deck, looking out at the forest as well. "He'll come back," she said, although for the first time, Megan could hear the unsure undertones in her friend's voice.

It had her glancing back at the forest one more time, just in case. The fear of not seeing him again was like a hungry little beast in her chest. It feasted on the turmoil inside, growing until it was wedged uncomfortably deep, making each breath hurt.

But she forced herself to remain positive. Fred was strong. He'd made it on his own for a long time. If any dog could outsmart an attacker, it was him.

Chapter Seventeen

✦❦✦

Staying the night with Crystal was just what Megan needed. Her house was airy and welcoming, with linen pillows on the couch and velvety rolled throws in decorative baskets. She definitely wasn't one to skimp on the finer details of decor. They ate a delicious dinner of shredded chicken in a sweet sauce, millet, and fresh greens.

Megan called and talked to her parents again, assuring them that things were going well and agreeing that they should come out in a week or two. It was a pleasant phone call, but she could tell they wanted to do more for her. It was clear they felt guilty for not supporting her move to Seacrest right away. So, when she got another phone call later that evening, she supposed it was them.

But instead, an unknown number from a Seattle area code appeared on her phone. She answered cautiously. The man on the other end was stiff and professional. He informed her she would be sent a link to join at 8 a.m. the next morning to give her statement regarding the hearing of Jarron Wallace. Then he thanked her, and their call came to a quick end.

"What was that?" Crystal asked, snuggled onto the couch.

Her eyes were wide, accentuating the pale blue color, similar to so many of the gems in her shop.

Megan sank into the down-stuffed cushions of the chair adjacent to her and dropped her phone on the fluffy carpet beside it, likely made from some rare type of alpaca wool. She gave her friend a fleeting smile as anxiety was already starting to build on top of the fears she had at the thought of making a statement. "It was a lawyer. I give my statement tomorrow morning."

"Oh, wow." Crystal tucked her knees up under a blanket and wrapped her arms around them. "But that's good, right? You'll get it over with quickly and then move on with your life."

"Yeah." Megan sighed. "I just don't know if this will ruin Jarron's life. That's not what I wanted."

"Of course not, but Megan." Crystal waited until Megan had looked back at her. "You're simply stating what happened from your point of view. That's it." She shrugged. "He was the one who chose to act that way."

"I know." Megan tried to ease the pricking sensation in her chest, but forcing herself to relax was nearly impossible. It just made her more tense.

"I, uh..." Crystal adjusted the blanket across her lap, pulling it tighter around her. "I saw Kenneth as he left your house tonight."

Her eyes lifted to settle on Megan, as if this were all she needed to say. But Megan wasn't sure where to go with her confession. She hardly knew what had happened between them herself. How could she explain it to someone else?

"And?" Megan finally asked, hoping for more. Maybe Kenneth said something or looked sad or angry. Anything.

Crystal's lip twitched into a smile. "And I've been mulling it over ever since. He looked a little traumatized. What happened between you two? What did you say?"

She hadn't said much of anything... it was more what they'd *done* that might be the problem. Megan crossed her legs and looked out at the window to the darkness beyond. During the day it framed the view of a small, fenced back-yard. The grass was green and full and it was neatly adorned with shrubs here and there, trimmed into spirals.

"I guess I was just overwhelmed by everything going on," Megan said quietly, thinking of Kenneth and the way he'd kissed her that night. Their first kiss that night had been slow and unexpected. Then the second evolved into something entirely different. He always seemed to be fighting an internal battle, one that pulled him to her and one that dragged him away. But then, so was she. Having just gotten away from Jarron, she didn't want a commitment, no matter how perfect the offer. But that was *her* dilemma. What was Kenneth afraid of?

Megan shook her head suddenly. "It's not what I need to be thinking about." She pulled her gaze from the dark window and back to Crystal. "There's at least one person that I know of searching out a black pearl necklace, and tonight mine was stolen. I believe someone framed Santiago, even though Kenneth thinks it's possible he was doing something to hurt his family's company. I'm not convinced about that."

"Have you actually spoken to his parents?" Crystal asked. Her eyes were drowsy, closing halfway as she waited out an answer. But to Megan, the thought of asking Mark and Carolina Fitch seemed out of the question. Don a costume and impersonate a client at an investing firm, sure. But approach the owners of Fitch Inc? That seemed a little over the top.

Megan finally shook her head and Crystal smiled. "Well, why not? They'd be the ones to know if they pressed charges for a proven reason or a speculated one."

She yawned and lifted the throw over her shoulders,

freeing her legs as she crawled to the other end of the couch. She pulled her phone from where it had been wedged between the cushions. "Sometimes I just stash my phone here because I know that's where it will end up, anyway."

She winked at Megan and situated herself again, holding her phone up expectantly. "Want me to call them?" She glanced down at the screen of her phone again. "It's only 10:00, and I happen to know they're night owls, so they will most definitely be up. What do you think?"

"You know their number?" Megan's thoughts were swimming a bit, meshing with the shock of being unconscious, having her house ransacked, and finally ending up in Kenneth's arms. She tried to focus on the moment at hand.

The memory of Santiago sitting in a jumpsuit behind a heavy plastic screen had her indecision clearing. "Let's call them."

Crystal's grin was a touch wicked, making her wonder suddenly if there were other motives to the spontaneous call. And if she'd had this power all along, why hadn't she reached out to them before now? But there was no time to ask. Crystal was already spouting off a cheerful greeting and a quick, bold question.

"Do you honestly believe Santiago was trying to sabotage your company?"

There was a quiet moment where Crystal gazed stony-faced at the floor. Then her eyes flickered to Megan's, and she pulled the phone from her ear, pressing a button. The call switched to speaker, and a woman's voice filled the room, rattling away quickly.

"... was really no concrete evidence. But the facts stated were fairly startling and by a very trusted advisor. He's known our family since the beginning, before there was any money to speak of. I know you have a powerful circle, Miss Chambers, believe me. But the last thing I want is venom from any of you. If we felt there were any other way to deal with this threat, we would have tried it first."

The pause that followed was jarring. Megan leaned forward slightly. "His mother?" she whispered. Crystal nodded, and then her eyes narrowed.

"And who was this trusted man?"

"His name is protected at this time," Mrs. Fitch said.

"I see," Crystal said. Her voice rang with power and, although Megan couldn't decipher how, wealth. "Perhaps you could tell me his occupation, then?"

"He was an appraiser at our company for many years, from the very beginning. And then to Santiago."

"And so you took the advice of this man?" Crystal asked, her words hot on the answer of Mrs. Fitch. "The man in the most likely position to blackmail your son?"

"You may not know, Miss Chambers, that Santiago attempted to slander this company before. His final chance was to succeed with these accounts in Switzerland and France—"

"And that was a secret, was it?" Crystal's voice echoed against the dark-stained beams of her vaulted ceiling. "No one else would see this as an opportunity to blacken his name and strip his power, thus stepping into his vacant space in the company?"

The overwhelming silence returned, and a smile crept across Megan's face. Her eyebrows lifted with admiration for her friend. She saw the flicker of a smile pull at Crystal's mouth.

"I know you love your son," Crystal said, her voice softening. "I'm just asking you to love him enough to explore the possibility that everything he told you... just might be true."

"I see what you're saying," Carolina said, "and I appreciate your concern. A family of your status has the benefit of demanding attention."

It sounded like a brush off. Megan could hear it, and she saw the proof of it in the downturn of Crystal's mouth. But after a brief pause, Mrs. Fitch's tone had change.

"I'll be sure to look into his associations. If anyone is remotely capable of this, I will find out. As you said, we need to be sure. I do love my son, Miss Chambers. Goodnight."

"Goodnight, ma'am." Crystal let her phone drop into the cushion again and released a heavy breath, sinking into the couch. "Let's hope she really means that."

"So." Megan sat up taller, although the sinking softness of the chair made it difficult. "You're saying you think someone who knew Santiago personally saw this opportunity to blackmail him?" She gazed thoughtfully at her friend. "That would narrow it down a bit."

"Yes, it would," Crystal said. "You know..." She pushed up on her elbows. "I should have just called them in the beginning. But they never knew me, they just knew *of* me. And if you hadn't become friends with Santiago, I still wouldn't know that he was *the* Santiago Fitch. Being separated from the pomp and glitter of it all was just so liberating. Here in Seacrest, I'm just..." She shrugged. "Crystal."

Megan's eyelids were heavy, and her head tilted in wonder. "So, who are you in the other life? You know, the glittery one." As she sat in the most luxurious chair she'd ever been in, Megan suspected Crystal hadn't shed quite *everything* from her former life.

"Well, ten years ago my dad was governor of Washington." Her matter-of-fact tone turned to laughter the moment she looked at Megan. "He was, okay?"

Megan gawked as her friend's name blared in her head. Chambers. Governor Chambers. "Of course," she murmured. "You're Chamber's Little Treasure."

"Oh gosh, don't remind me." Crystal groaned. "I hated

that nickname. It never left me. Everyone seemed to pick up on it the moment they heard it."

"Sorry." Megan grinned. "I won't say it literally every time we meet."

"No." Crystal's eyes widened seriously. "You *won't*."

Something disturbed the silence from outside, and Megan got to her feet. "Did you hear that?" She crossed the room quickly, looking out through a row of windows. There was only coastline glimmering in the moonlight. "Do you think that could have been Fred?"

"Sorry, Megan, but I really doubt it," Crystal said, although she stood and joined Megan at the window. "I've never seen Fred out here. We're pretty far from anything, which is why I went with such a high-tech security system."

"I wonder if we should check back at my house, just to be sure. What if he went home?" Megan couldn't stand the thought of Fred thinking she'd left him. It tore at her heart.

"Megan, you were attacked today," Crystal said. Her reflection in the window met Megan's eyes. "Now, I don't know why they simply left you behind and went on to destroy your house, but Kenneth knew what he was doing when he suggested you stay here or with him."

"I know why," Megan whispered.

She'd thought back to climbing down the cliff, and suddenly there were flashes of new memory. She remembered reaching for the hand that had covered her face and feeling a slender arm and a delicate bracelet.

"It was Lyanna. She would do anything for Cleopatra's necklace."

"The one who knocked you out?" Crystal asked. In her reflection, her eyes were open wide. Haunted, colorless voids. It made Megan shiver, and she shook her head. "I know it was, although I never saw her."

Crystal's reflection frowned. "Also, who's Lyanna, and did you say *Cleopatra's* necklace?"

Megan's tiredness vanished and she turned to Crystal. "Yes. Lyanna is the fiancée of one of Santiago's clients. She's obsessed with this legend of Cleopatra's necklace, and I met her. She must have looked into me and found out about the black pearls. And then she tore my house apart, which means she had to be the one who knocked me out." She turned her head to look at the real Crystal. "Doesn't it?"

Crystal's lips pressed together. "I guess it could. But what would she want with Fred?"

"We don't know that anyone has Fred," Megan said. "If you ask me, he just got frightened by all the destruction in the house and ran off."

"Either way, let's talk with the police chief in the morning." Crystal yawned. "It's been a difficult day for everyone, and maybe Fred will be back at home at sunrise."

"I hope so."

Their conversation drifted into silence, and the night wore on. Crystal slept in her room, and Megan took one of the guest rooms. She knew she should sleep, but the thought that Lyanna had actually pressed a chemical-soaked cloth to her face was unsettling.

She paced in front of the window, her mind on Santiago. There was so little time left before his hearing. Maybe if she could get some information on people who might have been close enough to him to know there was an opportunity for blackmail. The only person she knew how to contact would be his lawyer. Yost. She settled on the bed, leaned against the soft headboard, and stared out at the night. It seemed strange that Derek would be framed and fired. The lawyer to a blackmail case accused of blackmail. How ironic.

When her thoughts turned to Kenneth, her eyes closed. It

was the only way to fully relive their kiss. The way he'd held her was something she could get used to. The way he'd lowered to her so slowly. The first touch of his lips had been cautious. Sweet.

Her phone rang, and she jerked upright from where she'd fallen asleep in an uncomfortable slump, half sitting and curved over so that her head was nearly upside down. With one look at the time on her screen, her heart was racing. It was nearly 8 a.m.

"Hello?" Her voice was groggy, but she paid it no attention and slid out of bed.

An electronic voice followed, "Please be ready for your video call in 10 minutes. Your link has been sent to you. If you did not receive your link——"

She pulled her phone away and glanced at the screen, seeing she had a new text from the same number. She pressed her phone to her ear again.

"Thank you," the voice said.

Loud bells chimed in her ear, and she gasped, silencing the alarm on her phone. She must have set it wrong the night before. But if they were going to be recording her in ten minutes, she had to move fast.

She started in the bathroom, splashing her face with water and smoothing out her hair. The messiness had it looking like it might be naturally curly, so she went with it, scrunching some mousse into the *curls*. Her life felt abstract as she rushed through getting ready.

Had she really been attacked by Lyanna the day before and then robbed? It didn't seem real. Was she really about to make a statement against Jarron, her ex-fiancé who so worshiped other's opinions that he'd ask her to marry him? It was pitiful, she decided. But then, if he hadn't passed out the day he was at her parents' house, it could have been bad. She needed to take this stand against him, as horrible as she felt doing it.

When she was ready, she set up her laptop at the corner desk and connected her phone. Then she pressed the link she'd been given. It was exactly 8:02, and a grid of four screens appeared on her computer. In one, she saw herself, thankfully looking less nervous than she felt. There was one screen with a woman in a judge's gown. One screen had a woman who was dressed in a very professional suit and smiled back at her, and the last had her tensing up. Jarron stared back at her. A man next to him was tapping a paper on the desk, appearing to be explaining something. But Jarron didn't respond; his eyes only bored back at Megan. His gaze was harder than she was used to. No pretending. No manipulating. He was making a statement of his own. She could practically hear his voice in her mind, strong and threatening.

Just try it.

Chapter Eighteen

"Your statement, Ms. Henny?"

Megan tore her gaze from Jarron and looked at the robed woman, managing a small lift of her lips. She'd heard part of the introduction and an explanation of how the meeting would go, but mostly she was repeating the incident at her parents' house over and over in her mind as she stared wide-eyed back at Jarron. Would this ruin his career? Would he hate her forever?

She took a quick breath, stopping the panic from building. Neither of those potential outcomes were in her control, and none of this was her fault. She faced the judge again, whose name she'd completely missed.

"Yes." She took a deep breath. "This statement is true and recalled from the best of my memory. I went to my parents' house in Seattle just to check on things while they were out of town..."

She explained every moment, keeping her eyes on the judge and trying to ignore the fact that Jarron was listening. And watching. But when she explained the turn of his countenance, and the moment she knew he was going to physically attack her, she glanced at him.

His face was red, and his jaw muscles tensed as if he were clenching his teeth together. She turned back to the judge to finish her statement, but Jarron's voice roared out of her computer.

"She's lying! I don't remember any of this, and I've never hurt anyone in my life. She's just saying this to get back at me. Like she always does." His eyes bored into hers, pained and suffering.

The lawyer next to him was shaking his head and rattling away in Jarron's ear, but Jarron didn't listen.

"I don't know how, but she knows what she's doing. All of the sudden, they're talking about her. *Everyone.* She's the center of gossip in the most elite circles. People who should be *my* friends, but now all they do is shun me and whisper about her. Talking about how intriguing she is, that the spy from India has been hired to track her down. She's searching for Megan and a precious necklace. Santiago Fitch probably hired her." He slammed his hands down on the desk, shooting to his feet. "That's what you should be asking!"

His video cut out, and Megan realized her mouth had dropped open. There was nowhere to go with this information. How could she ever verify what he was saying? A spy had been hired? For *her*? She stared at her computer screen in shock.

"I'm so sorry about that, Ms. Henny," the woman lawyer said. "He never should have been able to speak out of turn like that. I believe the audio was set up incorrectly." She gestured with one hand. "Please continue with your statement. Did Mr. Wallace hit you?"

"Uh... No, but I think he was about to," Megan said. "He passed out as he attempted to reach for me."

The rest of the interview was brief. She was asked a few

questions, then told her that was all they needed. And it was over. Her screen flickered to a plain blue, and she gazed into it until her eyes ached.

There was a gentle knock on her door, and Crystal peeked in.

"How'd it go?" She was wrapped in a blush pink robe and took a few steps closer, seeming to be gauging Megan's face.

"Uh..." Megan wasn't sure what to say. "Jarron hates me, that's for sure."

Suddenly she remembered she was speaking to Crystal Chambers, the former governor's daughter. Surely, if there was some high-class gossip going around, she might have the right resources.

Her eyes lifted. "He said something crazy, but maybe you can help."

Crystal nodded and sat on the edge of the bed. "Go on."

"He claimed a spy from India had been hired to find me?" Megan shook her head. "Jarron claims whoever this person is, he's been hearing from his social circle that they're searching out a rare necklace. But that's crazy, isn't it?"

Crystal sighed, not looking as shocked as Megan had expected. In fact, she looked like she knew exactly what Megan was talking about. She nodded, and her eyes narrowed as if she were recalling something from long ago. "Espionage can sometimes be a friendly fight. In the world of politics, we win some, we lose some, but it doesn't have to go beyond that. It's hardly ever pursued to the end. It's just a game of manipulation, trying to win enough rounds to come out on top." She smoothed the length of her silky robe.

"I've heard of this person. She's just the type of profes-sional this Lyanna woman might turn to, actually. Her reputa-tion is incredible. I thought of her when you told me the story, but..." She shrugged, letting out a heavy sigh. "What are the odds? I mean, why come here of all places? Little Seacrest."

"Maybe she heard about my necklace—"

"No." Crystal shook her head. "That's not how this works. Spies can't just follow hunches and tips here and there and travel all over the world searching out the next rumor. It's scientific. If she were searching for this necklace, she would have started with the legend itself and worked through time and history. She would find accounts of where it disappeared and where it surfaced again. It's almost mathematical."

"And the odds of her landing here in Seacrest?" Megan asked.

"I would say it's impossible." Crystal said. "But you can't just ignore it, either. Maybe the impossible happened."

Suddenly Crystal stood and clasped her hands together. "Sorry to change gears, but I came in here to tell you the police are headed to your house in half an hour's time. Kenneth didn't get an answer from your phone, so he called mine."

"Oh." Megan closed her laptop and glanced down at her phone to see a missed call. "Well then, we'd better get going."

THE DRIVE TO HER HOUSE WAS UNEVENTFUL, ALTHOUGH SHE searched for Fred the entire time. Crystal drove, staying mostly quiet besides a casual comment here and there about the weather. It had turned breezy, with occasional gusts making the car swerve.

When they got to Megan's house, a police cruiser was there. The two officers inside the vehicle were looking intently at a computer screen, so Megan walked past them to check on Fred's food bowl first. It lay just as she'd left it, dog food untouched. But when she went to enter her house, she saw a paper had been folded up and jammed into the crease between the door and the frame. She pulled it out, opening it slowly.

Crystal had stayed in the car, saying she was going to make a phone call and then join her. So, Megan was alone when she began to read the small paragraph that had been scribbled out by hand.

I KNOW YOU HAVE THE NECKLACE I'VE BEEN SEARCHING FOR. IT is not yours. Once it's in my hands, I will return your dog. Patience is not a quality of mine, so I will give you until tonight at 10 p.m. Leave the necklace here on the porch where you've placed a blanket for Fred. If I don't have it in my hands by morning, you'll never see him again.

SHE LOOKED DOWN AT THE BLANKET TO SEE FRED'S COLLAR, his golden tag with his name on it facing her. Lowering to her heels, she picked it up.

"What's this?" Crystal stood next to her, reading over her shoulder. She brought her hand to her mouth, as if to silence a gasp, but there was no sound.

Megan rose to her feet. "I don't even know where to begin searching for him. Where would they take him?"

Crystal turned to the forest, and her eyes scanned the trees. "Anywhere," she said quietly.

"Crystal." Megan waited for her friend to turn around. She held up the note. "This means whoever searched my house never found the necklace. But if that's true, then where did it go?"

"Do you have any idea where it might have come from?" Crystal asked.

Megan shook her head. "None. Police ran a search for a few months, but nothing came up."

"Hmm." Crystal turned as boots tromped up the steps of the deck, and Megan stuffed the note in her pocket.

"Hello, Ms. Henny." The taller and older of the two policemen greeted her. He had deep brown hair with auburn streaks in it and dark brown eyes. He extended his hand, and she shook it firmly.

"I'm Sheriff Anderson," he continued, "this is officer Kellen." The younger officer had a very youthful face and bright blue eyes, but his blond hair was thinning severely. He touched his hat and offered a friendly smile. Sheriff Anderson glanced at her house with a tight shake of his head. "First your shop and now this. I'm sorry you've received such a rude welcome to the area. I assure you it isn't the way of things here."

"Thank you." Megan wasn't sure what to say. It had her feeling like she was somehow to blame for all the commotion in her life. Or was he simply giving her an apology? She chose to believe the latter as she followed him into her house.

The officers explored each room quietly, keeping the conversation between themselves. Megan and Crystal settled at the kitchen to watch and listen. But there wasn't much to overhear. They spoke about thieves of opportunity and childish pranks, and Megan couldn't help feeling frustrated.

She slid down from the barstool she was perched on and met them on their way out of the master bedroom. "Kenneth did send you pictures from yesterday, right?"

The sheriff nodded in one quick dip of his head. "Yes, ma'am. We've got 'em, and we'll be filing a report. He also said you were having a security system installed?"

"Oh." Megan had forgotten all about it. "That's right."

"That will help a lot with things like this. Someone wanting to cause trouble will just take one look at a window sensor or a security camera, and they won't want to mess with it."

"Sheriff Anderson." Megan folded her arms, looking between him and the younger officer. "I heard something just today that I wanted to ask you about."

The sheriff took a small step forward, as if he were eager to get going, but he kept a smile on his face. "And what was that?"

"I was told someone hired a professional to track me." She hesitated saying the word, but there was really no way around it. "A spy. Someone out of India searching for a necklace they believed me to have."

The sheriff's reddish-brown eyebrows rose. "Ah."

"She does exist," Crystal chimed in behind them. "I can vouch for that."

"Yes, yes, we know she exists." The sheriff rubbed his neck and glanced around the room.

Megan's arms dropped to her sides in shock.

"We're warned," he continued, "whenever someone of that, you know... *profession* might be in the area. It's critical for law enforcement to be aware, especially in a small town like this. Because you see..."

He looked uncomfortable, and his eyes met the younger officer more than once as if he were hoping for a way out of their conversation. Finally, he continued. "Well, if it's who I believe it is, she has diplomatic immunity."

"You can't be serious." Megan's irritation doubled. "She's a diplomat?"

He grimaced. "Yes, and a valuable one. Valuable enough that we've been warned not to take notice of her. She's been working with the US for years, and any side hustling she has going on, I was assured, is harmless." He stopped after glancing at Megan's incredulous expression and seemed to reconsider his course. "It's a long shot if she's responsible for the damage to your house. But if she was, what do you suppose she'd be looking for?"

Megan dug the crumpled note from her pocket and held it out. "My necklace."

His face hardened as he scanned the note quickly. "When did you find this?"

"Just this morning. It was here, slid into the door." Megan held her hand out, and he gave the note back. She lifted it up in front of them. "Do you know where she's staying?"

He rubbed his chin with a sigh. "No, ma'am." His gaze softened. "I'm sorry, but we can't touch this. And I need to caution you to stay away as well. Diplomatic immunity is nothing to mess with."

"But if she's done something illegal—"

"Then more than likely, she gets away with it." He touched his hat and made his way for the door. The smile had long since left his face. "I apologize."

"But she has my dog!" Megan's voice echoed through the house. "If you think I'm just going to let her steal him, you're wrong. But the problem is"—she walked to the doorway where he'd stopped just short of leaving—"someone took it." Megan shrugged. "I don't have the necklace anymore. So, what am I going to do?"

He sighed, but this time it was a breath of frustration. "Okay, I'll see what I can do. I know it's upsetting, but right now all you can do is wait. Just give me time to make some calls and do what I can to confirm that she's even still here." He shook his head. "They might not tell me anything. I'm just saying, I'll do what I can." His eyes bored into hers. "Don't do anything impulsive, I'm cautioning you. Wait for my call."

He looked from Megan to Crystal and stepped out the doorway. "Good day, ladies."

Pangs of disappointment gnawed at Megan's stomach. She stared out the doorway in silence for a time, thinking of Fred and his trust in her. She doubted Officer Anderson would be given the woman's location. And aside from combing the entire town of Seacrest and any outlying habitations as well, she had no way of finding her. But one thing she did know was that whoever had stolen him would return here to collect the necklace... and standing right next to her was an expert jeweler.

Megan turned to Crystal. "I know what to do," she said. "C'mon." Taking Crystal's hand, she towed her through the doorway and out onto the deck.

৩৯৫৩

SANTIAGO DIDN'T UTTER A WORD. HE ONLY LISTENED TO the sound of his mother offering an apology. Vague and self-gratifying, but still an apology. It was a big step in their relationship. When she'd finished explaining the mechanics of her apology, there was a pause, a silence he understood was an allowance for him to express his gratitude.

He took a slow breath, contemplating the variety of responses in his mind. Should he drudge up the past or let things start anew from this moment? Or should he ignore both and challenge her, demanding to know her strategy? She was a loving mother, sure. But more distrustful of others than anyone he'd ever met. Even her own son didn't garner exception.

"Son."

His mother had grown weary of waiting. It was a character fault she refused to admit. But as she continued, her voice became gentler.

"I know things have been difficult for you, and you feel we've judged you too quickly and too harshly. But you know what it takes to run a successful empire like ours. It's war. Whispers of ambush must be taken seriously. *We* must be taken seriously. And to do that, we need to pursue any possibility of espionage while also keeping away from negative, high-profile gossip.

Santiago sat up from his slouched position, and the metal chair squeaked beneath him. "High-profile gossip," he repeated. "So, who's doing the gossiping?"

Silence.

"You know." Santiago twisted the cord of the phone in one hand. "I told you in the beginning, there were pieces that had been switched out. They were fakes. You asked me then, why I didn't tell you right away. Well, this is why. You don't talk to me, and you've trained me from a young age not to talk to you."

He ran a hand through his hair. It was dirty, as it always was now. Showers weren't allotted as often as he would prefer, and a single bar of soap was all he'd been given. "So, I ask you now, as a plea for your trust. Who's doing the gossiping? What have you heard? Because my future is not the only one being threatened."

He sat through the silence more comfortably now, awaiting her decision to take his olive branch or not. It was up to her how their lives interconnected from this moment on.

"Do you remember Governor Chamber's daughter?" she asked.

"You're talking about Crystal Chambers?"

"Yes." His mother's voice was slightly rigid, but he attributed that to her inexperience with allowing him into the details of her life. "She called me abruptly, asking about your case and claiming you could have been blackmailed by those close to you. Those who knew of our slight estrangement within the company."

"I see," he said, waiting for her to continue.

"And we've heard some rumors since she called. Rumors

that tell me there's more going on than we might have suspected."

"What rumors?" She didn't answer right away, and he glanced at the clock. They wouldn't be given much more time to talk.

"Rumors that Aralyn had been sent to Seacrest. Do you remember her? A diplomat and spy from India who knows more about the jewelry trade than anyone I've ever met, myself included. I hired her many years ago under the alias of Dominique, although she has more names than those."

"Do you know what she's doing here?" he asked.

His mother sighed before answering, which he knew meant she was going to tell him but would rather not.

"It is believed she was hired by two individuals at different times. One recently, who happens to be a client of yours, Carter Dewald."

Santiago tensed as worry for Megan filled his mind. He'd heard about her paying a visit to his office and wouldn't put it past Dewald to retaliate. But if this spy had been hired to find the same necklace that Dewald had asked Santiago to find, she would have started at the beginning just as he had. She would have found that the last known resting place for the pearls of Cleopatra was in London. Nothing would have led her to Seacrest... so why was she there?

"And the other is lesser known," his mother continued. "I only hear it's a young man who's been working with her for a couple of years. To be honest, I thought it might be you."

"Me?" The door to his booth opened, and Santiago continued quickly. "Why?"

"Because she would easily be able to exchange the authentic pieces for fakes, and no one would ever know. I assumed you'd hired her because, in a way, that would keep her loyal to our family. I mean, how could she accept a job that double-crosses her own clients?"

"Mom, she's a criminal."

A hand reached forward and pushed down the receiver on the old phone, ending their call.

"Time's up, kid."

Santiago barely had time to replace the phone before the guard with a swollen gut pressing against his uniform buttons and a shiny bald head clamped onto his arm and dragged him out of the room. "Back to your cell. Let's go."

Santiago tuned it out, all of it. He knew he'd done nothing to belong there and to warrant such treatment, but there was no getting out of it. So, he simply endured and attempted, as much as possible, to separate his mind from the treatment of his body. It could be much worse; he was fully aware.

But for now, when he was pushed into his cell even after showing no resistance and carefully following every order, he let the disparaging treatment roll off his back like morning dew on a duck's oil-infused feathers. He told himself it was nothing to him. But somehow it still managed to steal a fragment of his dignity with every offense.

Before the guard was out of view, he shouted out a request to contact his lawyer. It was met with a roll of the big guard's shoulders. He hoped that was a yes, because something told him he was running out of time.

Chapter Nineteen

"So, where are we going?" Crystal snuck a few sideglances Megan's way. "And why do your eyes look so wild?"

Megan eased up on the accelerator, having noticed the speed was inching up right along with her tension. She tried to calm down, but it was difficult. She could only think of Fred and how to get him back. She took a quick breath and looked at her friend. "I know how to trick this spy into giving us Fred back."

"You do?" Asked Crystal.

Megan slowed down even more, glancing a little deeper into Crystal's eyes. "We're going to make a black pearl necklace. Or, I guess you are. But I can help. What do we do? Where do we go?"

Crystal gazed out the window with wide eyes, taking a moment to respond. "Head to my shop on the boardwalk," she said, giving Megan a smile. "Everything we need should be there."

At the boardwalk, shops were open, and tourism was

going strong. Megan took the little red hatchback down the alleyway. They parked at the back of Crystal's store and made their way inside. "Let's leave the main lighting off, that way people won't be confused thinking the shop is open," Crystal said.

"OK, how fast can we do this?" Megan was practically shaking with anticipation.

Crystal took a moment before answering and pulled various tools out of the drawers. She set two different sized paint brushes on the workbench, along with a basket containing a dozen bottles of paint and needle-nose pliers. Then she dug into a large tote, pulling out coils of plastic string, and containers of beads. "This should do it," she said. "It won't take long at all. We only need to worry about giving the paint enough time to dry. If it's streaked or smudged, she'll be able to tell right away. We need to give ourselves a window of opportunity before she realizes it's a fake. And she *will* realize it. Here."

She handed Megan a paintbrush and a jar of black enamel paint and scooted a plastic container across the workbench. "Get started on the first coat. It doesn't matter how good it looks, it's just a base color." She gave Megan an encouraging smile and began measuring out the plastic string.

Megan shook the jar and got to work. It was more time-consuming than she'd expected, but eventually she used the technique of threading a toothpick through the hole of the bead and then painting went much quicker. She moved from bead to bead, sitting them carefully on a paper towel to dry when she was finished. As she worked, she watched Crystal configure small pieces of metal and mount them onto one end of the string.

"So Crystal," she said, "what have things been like since your dad moved on from being governor?"

Crystal gave her a wry smile. "You mean since he was voted out? Things have actually been much better. He went on to get a job at Harvard, teaching at the John F. Kennedy School of Government. I think he really enjoys it. Or, at least, he seems to. He's been working there ever since."

"Ten years of teaching at Harvard," Megan mused. "Seems like he would have some stories to tell. Does he ever meet any celebrity students? Or their children?"

"He hears all the gossip and has met more people with well-known names than when he was governor," Crystal said, lifting the string up and giving it a snip with a small pair of scissors. "But lately I haven't heard from him as often as usual. When I first came out to Seacrest, I received a call almost daily, and then weekly... and now it's been over a month since I last got a phone call. I imagine he's busy. But to be fair, nothing is stopping me from giving *him* a call too."

"He should come out to Seacrest sometime," Megan said. "I would love to meet him."

Crystal gave her an appreciative glance. "I'll tell him that," she said. "I'm sure he would love to meet you too." She leaned over to gaze at the small pile of beads that were drying on the paper towel. "These look good, but we'll have to do two more coats of paint before we start threading them."

She picked up another jar from the basket and began shaking it. This one was a blue-black color that looked like it would have a very similar shine to the real black pearls on Megan's necklace. Taking up a paintbrush, Crystal began giving the beads that had dried a second coat, as Megan continued working on the first coat. Gradually their small pile of painted beads grew.

"One time, my dad called me with some... well, some pretty terrifying news." Crystal smoothed a brush of paint over another bead as she spoke. "He said he'd found a device underneath his car. It was screwed right onto the frame, and he called the police right away."

She paused her work and looked up at Megan. "When police arrived, they determined it was a bomb." She shook her head. "Can you believe it? Someone actually tried to have my dad killed. It's so hard to understand why anyone would do something like that. Especially when he's only a teacher. What could possibly drive them to such extreme behavior?"

"Who knows?" Megan paused and looked out across the beautiful little jewelry shop. "That's shocking, though, absolutely. It seems to me a threat like that says more about the one doing the threatening than it does about anyone else. Did they ever figure out who put it there?"

"No, unfortunately." Crystal sighed and looked back at Megan with a shrug. "I'm just glad it never happened again. That was over two years ago, and it's been pretty smooth sailing since then."

"Well, I'm glad to hear it." Megan completed one final brushstroke on the last bead and placed it on the paper towel. "I, for one, appreciated his efforts on wilderness preservation. It's one of the few things I believe gets more important with each passing year."

"He would wholeheartedly agree with you." Crystal paused, and a smile flickered across her face. "You know, I think I'll give him a call this weekend. It's been too long since he's had a break, and I think he would really love a weekend out here at Seacrest."

She continued painting but tilted her head toward an old desk with half a dozen drawers. "Can you look through those drawers and try to find a clear bottle of finishing enamel? That's our last step, and then we'll be ready to go."

"Sure," Megan said, making her way over to the desk. She started at the top left drawer and made her way down, finding mostly empty compartments. But at the third attempt, there was a stack of letters with Crystal's name written on the front. They were tied in pink ribbon with a bow on top, as if they were very special. It had her curiosity tingling. Before she closed the drawer, Megan glanced to the top left corner, but there was no return address. She closed the drawer and kept searching, pushing the revelation to the back of her mind for another time.

At the second to last drawer, there were four clear bottles of enamel paint. She pulled them out, about to bring them to Crystal. Then out of curiosity, she opened the very last drawer. But there was only dust. The envelopes were the most interesting thing, aside from stray pencils and a ruler. Her thoughts suddenly turned to Kenneth, and she tensed at the idea. If Crystal were harboring feelings for him, surely she would have mentioned it the night of the fundraiser. She brought the paint to Crystal and stood there hesitating.

Crystal glanced at the bottles. "Those are perfect, thank you," she said without looking up from her work, continuing her gentle brush strokes over the beads.

Megan plunked down in the stool next to her. It was no use. She had to know. "Who are all those letters from in your desk drawer?"

She watched as Crystal's eyes slowly lifted from her project to meet Megan's.

"I, uh, just noticed them as I was looking for the paint," Megan explained. "They're tied in a ribbon, which makes me think they're important." She gave her friend the smallest smile, hoping to encourage an answer out of her.

Setting her paintbrush aside, Crystal scooted back from the table and for a moment, she said nothing. Then she took a slow, steady breath as if the memory were very sweet but also possibly painful.

"Well, they are very special," she said. "Someone sent me

those letters about five years ago. It was right before I moved here to Seacrest, and I just wasn't sure about a relationship at that time. He was very devoted, and he listened to me when I asked him not to come visit."

Her expression saddened and she shrugged. "But, I kind of wish he hadn't." She scooted back to the table. "But anyway, I let him go, and I'm sure by now he's married with a kid or two and living happily without me. Who knew that little bit of distance I asked for was going to last forever? I never would've guessed it."

She turned back to Megan suddenly. "In this day, if someone takes the time to send you handwritten letters instead of a simple text, don't let them go. It's a rare find, and I don't think I'll ever meet a man like that again."

"I'm sorry to pry," Megan said, feeling a little guilty for Crystal's pain. "What was his name?"

Crystal began brushing a clear-coat atop the pearls. "Actually, it's nice to have someone to talk to." Her head tilted to the side as she continued, "His name was Andrew. An artist, he was commissioned to do several paintings at the time for some of the office buildings going up in Spokane. But his day job was in finance. He always said one job paid the bills, and the other filled his soul."

"He sounds nice," Megan said.

They sat in silence while Megan imagined what Crystal's life might have been like if she'd said yes to Andrew so long ago. But then, she was glad to have such a good friend at Seacrest.

"Really, it's okay. I'm fine." Crystal stood, crossing her arms as she looked down at the finished beads. "It's just that his letters say so many sweet things. I just couldn't throw them away."

She looked up at Megan and nodded, as if that were the end of it. But Megan couldn't help wondering just where this

Andrew had gone, and if he still thought of Crystal too. She would bet he hadn't moved on nearly as quickly as Crystal seemed to think. Still, it was strange that he would simply stop contacting her when, by the looks of those letters, he'd been so in love.

"I thought when I moved here, that Santiago might be someone I could see myself with." Crystal smiled. "But in the end, we never really clicked the way you did with him." Her eyes strayed to Megan's. "You two clearly have a very close connection. I've enjoyed seeing the way he admires you. It would be good for a free spirit like him to have a stable person like you in his life."

"Yes." Megan adjusted in her chair, feeling a little uncomfortable. "But we're only friends. It's never been more than that. I've hoped to spend some time to myself and get things settled."

She turned back to the table where the beads looked like they had dried. "Honestly, I need this time to work on me. Plus, I still don't have a shop. I mean, I do, but it's just an empty building right now. Who knows what I'm going to even do with it?"

"Don't worry." Crystal picked up the plastic string and began threading the pearls through it, holding it up so that they could slide to the end. "We'll think of something. I like your idea about starting with sandwiches. It's simple, and no one else on the boardwalk is doing it."

She gave Megan a quick smile and added the last bead. Then, she began working on the final clasp. "Just start with that maybe, and see what else you can think of. At least it could pay the bills for now."

Megan thought about that, agreeing that sandwiches would be an easy start. She watched as Crystal finished the clasp and connected the two ends. Then she held it up in front of Megan. "Here we go," she said. "One black pearl necklace."

Megan held her hand out and Crystal laid the necklace across her palm. She closed her fingers around it gently and looked up at her friend. "Here we go."

Chapter Twenty

Megan adjusted the camping chair she was tucked into. Hidden away underneath the deck, she sat quietly next to Crystal. The wood planks were low, so she had to scoot down in her chair, hunkered into the canvas. But it gave her a view of the spaces between the slats where Fred's blanket and the newly fabricated black pearl necklace lay.

She knew it wouldn't fool a professional eye, but she didn't need to fool anyone. All she needed to do was get this woman close enough, then the pepper spray strapped to her hand would do the talking. Her temperature rose when she thought of the note and how the woman had dared to threaten Fred. But at least she knew where he was... sort of. And she knew he was safe, for now.

Seeing as how it was only late afternoon, they had a while to wait. Crystal was busy scrolling through her emails and online orders since she'd spent so much time away from her work lately helping Megan.

Megan adjusted in her seat and pulled out her phone too, searching through the few pages of apps and trying to select the right distraction. But when she went to the last page, her finger hovering over the screen. There was an extra page, although she was very sure she'd never added it. Likely, her phone had updated and added the page automatically.

She swiped to the extra page. It could have been just an automatic thing, or a button she'd pushed once and never realized it had duplicated a page. But if that was the case... why was there a new folder sitting in the middle of the screen? Under the folder was the word *untitled*, and she knew she never would have added a folder without a name. Hesitating for a few seconds, she finally tapped the empty folder. An image popped up, and she gasped. It was the scorpion icon she'd seen on Derek's phone. The one he claimed he knew nothing about; the one Yost fired him for having.

"What is it?" Crystal whispered, leaning over to look at Megan's phone with her.

"I didn't put this here." Megan clicked the scorpion, and it opened to reveal five audio recordings.

"Oh my gosh," Crystal said. "What are those?"

Megan tapped the first one and heard voices, but not loud enough to make out what they were saying. She carefully turned the volume up, and chills ran though her body as she recognized her own voice. It was her conversation with Kenneth at his house, talking about dinner and then the envelope.

She clicked on each one, hearing more of the same. Her own voice having casual conversations with those around her. Crystal was in the third conversation, and her friend's pale blue eyes narrowed. The last recording had Megan's hand settling over her parted lips. It was not her voice, but someone new. A woman with a beautiful accent that lifted at the end of each word, her voice coated in smooth tones. She knew that voice. She remembered it. At the black-tie event, it was the stranger who'd commented on her necklace.

Megan turned to Crystal. "I know this woman. The one who came up to me that night at the party. Do you remember her?"

Crystal frowned, shaking her head. But when the voice continued, Megan's eyes widened. "We're in the yacht. I remember now. This was just before I passed out."

Crystal held her phone up, showing the voice memo screen to Megan as she pushed record. Megan gave her a thumbs-up.

"... *don't mean you any harm, of course. But I appreciate you leading me to Santiago's office. He always was eccentric.*"

There was the mumbled sound of Megan's voice as she tried to respond.

"*What? Well, according to the audio we just listened to, you have something I want. This isn't how I would normally do things, but you see, it's just too much of a coincidence. And in my world, more than one coincidence in one place is called fact.*"

Megan's voice groaned lightly in the background.

"*It's incredible really, the turns of fate.*"

There was a sigh and the creaking of leather, as if the woman had sat down. Her voice continued, fading in and out. It gave Megan the impression that her attacker was glancing around the room.

"*To imagine that you would buy the house that had been vacant for years. A decade, was it? If you look back even further, you'd see that the original owner of the house was the only owner. He never left and never sold. I'm assuming he died somewhere out at sea. Before moving here, he was a history nut who practically lived in the stacks of the London public library. He only went out once in a while, including the time he attended a rare-artifacts auction at the history museum.*

"*A necklace was purchased anonymously for six million dollars at that auction, but no one ever knew who the buyer was. Shortly after,*" *this house was built in Seacrest. Again, I'm sorry you became tangled in such a tale."*

The audio cut out and the app closed, returning to its hidden spot in a seemingly empty folder.

"Oh my gosh," Megan breathed. *The necklace was real?*

"What do you think—" Crystal began, but stopped when Megan held a finger to her lips.

She had no idea if the scorpion icon recorded at random or if it required a trigger. But if their conversations were being recorded, she didn't want to give away anything else. She pressed on the app and waited for a delete option, but nothing happened. She tried again, with no luck.

Crystal held her hand out, and Megan handed her the phone, watching as she navigated into settings. She clicked and clicked, down a weblike maze into her phone's deepest firewall layers. She clicked one final time, and there was the scorpion. She held her finger on it, and the image shook. Finally, there was a small x in the corner. A delete option. She pressed it, and the scorpion vanished.

Something rustled in the trees beyond the deck, and they both froze. A shape moved past the cracks between the stairs. She could see the outline of the woman she'd met. Her attacker. The woman who'd called herself Sylvia. Megan ground her teeth together, thinking of the cloth pressed to her face. She clasped her hands together as Sylvia came closer. The woman's expression was visible now as she stopped and folded her arms, staring at the deck. Poised. Controlled. She lowered slowly and took the fake necklace.

"Hello, beautiful," Sylvia said. She scanned the area carefully.

Megan glanced at Crystal. She was biting her lip, but she shook her head at Megan. Sylvia glanced around quietly for a moment longer and then turned, heading down the trail. Megan guessed she'd parked along the road and was going to cut through the forest. Wherever she was headed, it would lead to Fred.

Megan slid off her camping chair and snuck forward. Crystal grabbed her arm, and she turned around.

"I'm going to get Fred," she said, already feeling the tears welling in her eyes.

Her friend's expression was defiant, but she only stared back silently. With a huff of surrender, Crystal nodded and followed her out from under the deck.

Sylvia had disappeared, but she'd been headed north up the coastline and deeper into the forest. The trail was darkest there, snaking through dense pines. Megan held Crystal's hand behind her as she walked forward as silently as possible. The leaves were damp and quiet, for which she was grateful. But with each step, she imagined Sylvia emerging from the brush, and she struggled to push the fears away. Sylvia was likely thinking of what was ahead of her, not what might come from behind. Who was Megan to attempt tracking an internationally renowned spy, anyway? No doubt Sylvia hadn't given her a second thought. Especially when she'd been so easy to sneak up on the first time.

Megan caught a glimpse of something moving and stopped suddenly, bracing herself when Crystal collided with her. They held on to each other as they watched Sylvia on the trail ahead of them. Suddenly a light illuminated their surroundings. Sylvia's back was to them as she shone a light into the brush. Megan held her breath.

The beam of light came from Sylvia's phone, and she panned the area in front of her until finally choosing a direction. She plunged into the tall ferns, brushing aside a low pine bough. Water droplets showered down from the branch.

Sneaking forward, Megan only thought of Fred. Just what kind of condition was he in? Was this woman taking care of him, or was he locked away in a dark, cold space? She pushed aside the branch still swaying back and forth and charged into the forest. The street was closer here, she could tell. The lights of a passing car glowed through the branches and bushes as it cruised down the highway. Feeling desperate, Megan hurried forward. It had to be close.

"Megan, be careful!" Crystal whispered. Her voice was farther behind than Megan expected. Still, she pushed herself harder. There was a clearing only a few steps away.

Megan's foot caught on a root, and she fell hard. But as she looked up, she saw Sylvia along the road. The door to a small black car was open, and she looked up at the trees as if she'd heard Megan fall. It was too late. Before she could get to her feet, the car was pulling away. It made a U-turn and sped north, up the coastline again. Megan's breath rasped through her lungs, and her heart beat against her ribs.

"Are you okay?" Crystal held her arms as she stood, providing more comfort than help.

"Where is he?" Megan gasped. "How will I find him?"

"C'mon," Crystal said, pulling on her arm again. "We know what the car looks like, let's just drive down the coast and see if we can find it."

There was little hope in Megan's heart, but it was all they could do. She started to run, ignoring the whip of each branch she passed.

They made it back to Megan's car and sped down her drive to the highway. Megan peeled out and raced along the coastline. It was the steepest, most dangerous part of the scenic drive. Vacationers adored it. But at the speed Megan was approaching, it was terrifying, even to her. Still, she refused to slow down.

The road turned abruptly, and she slammed on the brakes. Crystal gripped the door handle with a quick intake of breath.

"Sorry," Megan said, slowing as she noticed tire tracks

along a dirt road to one side. The forest was sparser there, and she made out the dim glow of a porch light between the trees. It was far back from the road, nestled in darkness. But if she turned down the drive, her headlights would shine directly at it. She was stalled in the middle of the street, and she glanced at Crystal to see she was looking at the small house too.

"I'll just pull off the road here and walk out," Megan said, "just to get a closer look." Crystal looked like she wasn't happy with the idea, but she only watched as Megan switched off the headlights and pulled to the side of the road.

Stepping out of the car, she pressed the door closed as quietly as possible. An owl deep within the forest hooted a deep, repetitive call, and it echoed across the sky. Taking one slow step at a time, Megan approached the house. The tire tracks didn't lead to it, but instead circled around behind, out of view. She looked for a fence or chain where a dog might be kept and listened for any sound at all. But the surrounding area was deathly still. Too quiet. The only sounds of forest critters were from far beyond the little home. It made her feel exposed, as if her presence there was no secret.

The closer she got, the more she saw of the home. But it turned out to be more like a shed. And whether or not the tire tracks were from that evening, it didn't look like anyone was inside the building now. She peered in through a low window, seeing shadowy outlines of a chair and table. A refrigerator was up against one wall, and a small sink stood next to it.

A car engine roared to life, and she stumbled back from the window. Headlights flashed across her face, blinding her. Blocking the light with one hand, she peered at the vehicle. It was coming from behind the house and was much bigger than the one Sylvia had driven. But it wasn't until it stopped in front of her and someone got out that she was really worried.

She glanced back at her car, seeing Crystal had turned the headlights back on and was standing aside it.

"Megan?" Desmond appeared, walking up to her. He blocked the glare of the headlights with his lanky form. His bushy hair looked bigger than usual with the light beaming around him, and suddenly she recognized the food truck. Margaret got out of the driver's side.

Megan's breath released in a single gust. "Yes," she gasped. "It's me."

"Well, what on God's green earth?" Margaret's voice pierced the evening, and she walked carefully on the uneven ground, making her way to Megan. "What are you doing all the way out here? You need help?"

"No," Megan was still breathing hard. She looked back at Crystal and waved a hand to assure her she was okay. "I was actually looking for Fred."

"Oh no, not Freddie boy." Margaret's face was concerned, and in the backlit shadows, it was a haunted sight. She turned to Desmond. "I told you I heard barking, Dessie."

"It's Desmond, Gram," The young teen's voice was humdrum, and he shook his hair out of his face as he spoke.

"Well, I don't know what he'd be doing way out here," Desmond said. "But dogs are loud. It could have been miles away."

"It was right over there, I remember." Margaret pointed closer to the road, north of them. "I've never heard it before, and I thought it was strange, that's all I'm saying, Des— Desmond. And here comes Ms. Megan to tell us Fred is missing. What else am I to think?"

Desmond brushed his hair back and grunted small enough that it could have been an agreement or counter argument. It was difficult to tell. But Margaret seemed pacified.

She turned to Megan. "So tell me, is that all you came out here for?"

"Well, yes," Megan glanced around them, seeing Crystal had decided to join the party. She was walking toward them carefully in the dark, having reached the halfway point. "I thought I saw him come this way, and so we started driving." She looked in the direction Margaret had pointed.

"Well, you caught me in my secret lab." Margaret laughed at herself, not giving anyone time to guess the seriousness of her statement. "Your donuts are such a hit, I decided to make some of my own and see how the business does. You left your recipe on the counter, you know." She looked a little ashamed. "Was it terrible of me to take it?"

"Oh no, of course not," Megan tried to reassure her while scouring the area for any other tire tracks besides the food truck. There didn't appear to be another building close by. Sylvia wouldn't simply leave Fred out in the woods alone, would she? The threat on the note was haunting her thoughts and had her pulse quickening. She had to find him *now*.

"Thank you so much, dear." Margaret clasped Megan's hand in both of hers, and Megan turned back to her. "I want to tell you how sincerely I appreciate your help. I know this Santiago business has been on your mind, and that it's taken away from your own shop and livelihood. It's so kind of you to put your own welfare aside to help your friends."

Crystal stood close by, watching with an uneasy smile touching her lips.

"Thank you," Megan said, squeezing Margaret's hands. "It's been my pleasure. I love cooking, and as far as Santiago goes... I've gotten rather tangled in his affairs, actually. At first, I simply wanted to help, and now I don't have much of a choice."

Margaret's expression drooped, and her eyes darkened, matching the shadows around them. "You're not saying this is connected to Fred going missing, are you?"

"I'm afraid it is." Megan's heart throbbed, and she knew

they needed to keep going. No doubt Sylvia was already five steps ahead.

"Oh my." Margaret turned around, looking back toward where she'd claimed to hear barking. "I wonder..." She didn't finish her thought and only turned to each face, one after the other. Finally, she looked into Megan's eyes. "I haven't heard anything this evening."

"Don't worry about it," Megan assured, glancing back at her car. "I'll go explore the area down this way. Are there any other houses or buildings around here?"

Margaret frowned. "No, nothing close by. There is a sort of ranger storage shed." She tipped her head in the same direction as she'd pointed to earlier. "That way. About a mile up the road."

Megan hugged Margaret quickly and even pulled Desmond into a quick squeeze, which the young teen stiffened at. "Thank you both," she said, rushing back to the car with Crystal at her side.

"I have a feeling that ranger shed would be the perfect hiding place," Crystal whispered. Chills trailed down Megan's arms, and she took a deep breath, trying to calm her sudden jitters. She could feel the cold, mountain air on her widened eyes as she turned back to Crystal.

"Me too."

Chapter Twenty-One

There hadn't been another car on the road from the moment they'd left her house, but Megan couldn't help checking the rearview mirror every few seconds. She couldn't shake the feeling that someone was watching them. Her foot eased off the gas as they approached a break in the crowded forest.

She hadn't turned the headlights on since they'd left Margaret and Desmond, but thankfully the night was clear, and the moon gave off a silvery glow. Silhouettes were easily made out, and when she spotted an electrical hookup just off the road, she stopped quickly. She eased her car under a canopy of pine branches, assuring it wouldn't be seen by any passing drivers.

"Okay," Megan said, taking a steady breath. Crystal's hand was on the handle of her door, but she didn't get out. "You don't have to come if you don't want to." Guilt was tugging at Megan's mind. "You're not involved in this. I am."

"Well." She looked like she wanted to agree, but after turning to Megan, she shook her head. "How about I circle around wide, watching things, and call the police if I have to?"

Megan nodded and opened her door. There was no more time. She snuck forward, keeping away from the clearing. A small wooden shed came into view with a wire leading from the roof to a metal pole next to it. An electrical hookup. She watched for a moment before suddenly catching movement in the trees across the clearing. It was Crystal as she edged around the other side.

As the back of the structure came into view, she found a small car. It looked identical to the one Sylvia had gotten into. But where was Fred? Creeping forward more slowly, she left the cover of trees and began to cross the clearing. Her feet padded silently across layers of pine needles. Reaching the back of the shed, she eyed the back door. There were two cement steps leading up to it, and a light glowed dimly through the window. Aside the steps was a metal stake with a chain attached to it.

Something crashed inside the building, like dishes on the floor. The objects continued to scatter inside while a voice shouted. It was Sylvia. Megan's heart pounded, and she took a step closer to the door.

A bark shook through the house, and Megan held her breath.

Sylvia's voice rang out again, and she realized the woman was using her native language. But the message came across loud and clear. She wasn't happy with whatever was going on.

The door handle shook as the lock clicked. Megan dashed around the corner of the shed just as it swung open. Sylvia's voice was quieter now but still complaining. It had to be Hindi she was speaking, but in the middle of it all, Megan recognized one word. Fred. His loud breathing was such a comfort that she wanted to cry. He was alive, and he was here... and she was going to take him back.

A chain rattled, and Megan waited. Maybe she would just chain him up and go back inside. Or she might drive off somewhere. She wondered if Fred could smell her, as things seemed to be settling by the sound of it. Sylvia was quiet, and Fred breathed softer. But Megan also heard sounds she didn't recognize, like the clanking of delicate objects. Something small.

She leaned carefully to the edge of the building.

"Megan!" Crystal screamed, her voice shrill and panicked, and suddenly Megan knew what was happening. She burst around the building to see Sylvia with a syringe in her hand, holding a handful of Fred's coat in the other.

Sylvia jerked back in shock, dropping the syringe. It fell to the concrete step and broke. Jumping to her feet, she lunged at Megan. In a flash of movement, Sylvia's leg swiped both feet out from under Megan, who fell back hard, landing with the woman's forearm at her throat.

Fred erupted, barking viciously. He pulled at the chain, teeth bared. But it was too short, giving him only a few feet of movement. His barks rang out, echoing against the treetops.

"You knew the deal," Sylvia said. Her voice was harsh and threatening. "Where's the necklace?" Her arm eased up slightly, and Megan pulled in a raspy breath.

"I don't know where it went," she wheezed, "It disappeared the night you searched my house. I thought you took it."

Sylvia's gaze burned into Megan as if searching out the truth of her words. "Answer me one thing," she said. "How many pearls were on it?"

Megan knew what she was looking for. She knew the numbers and what they meant. Eight-five meant it was just a standard string of expensive pearls. Eighty-four meant a world of difference... and hers had eighty-four. She'd counted them that night after hearing the legend, disbelief causing her to count them again. And yet again.

"It has eighty-five," she lied, looking into Sylvia's charcoal eyes and seeing them flash with anger.

Whatever skills she had, Megan assumed detecting a lie was one of them. Plus, she wasn't a particularly skilled liar, which could be both a curse and a blessing. Today it was a curse.

"Where I'm from, lies become death." Her gaze narrowed. "If I don't have them, and you don't have them... where are they?"

Megan had no idea how to answer. Nothing she could think of would satisfy this woman; she was sure of that. "I don't know," she finally said.

Sylvia stood suddenly, dragging Megan up with her. "I'm not a criminal," she said, her voice grinding with anger. "I am a professional. I've been offered two million for this necklace, and I always deliver on my contracts. One million is already in a secured account." She paused, and her gaze softened. "But the other million is yet to be paid. If you tell me where the necklace is, I could split the remaining profit with you, fifty-fifty."

"I don't know where it is," Megan repeated. "But I can help you search for it."

Sylvia scoffed. "Please. You couldn't even sneak up on me when you had every advantage."

She had a point, but it was no matter. Megan's eyes wandered back to Fred. "Look, all I want is my dog back."

"And you can have him." Sylvia released her with one quick step back, still out of reach of Fred. His teeth were bared, and a growl vibrated in his throat, but he'd stopped barking. "As soon as you give me the necklace."

Something moved behind Sylvia, and Megan kept her eyes

on the spy in front of her, refusing to turn her gaze to Crystal as she crept forward.

"It was in my house before I went to the yacht, and then it was gone. Also, someone placed a recording virus on my phone. I assume it was you?"

Sylvia's eyes narrowed. But just as she looked about to respond, Crystal swung a branch, hitting her in the back of the head. Sylvia collapsed, face-first into the pine needles.

"Hurry," Megan said, rushing to release the chain. Fred licked her face, whining with happiness. "Hey, boy." She rubbed his coat as she pinched at the chain repeatedly. Finally, it fell away from his collar just as Sylvia began to stir.

Crystal grabbed her arm, and they fled with the Great Dane out in front. He dashed straight to the car, where he waited impatiently, whimpering and prancing on his feet.

"I know," Megan said, "we're going." She opened the door for him, and he dove in.

"She's coming." Crystal buckled up in the passenger seat and pointed a shaking hand out Megan's window. Megan glanced back to see Sylvia sprinting toward them. Starting the car, she pressed on the gas, peeling into a U-turn and speeding back down the highway.

"Where will we go?" Crystal asked, looking behind them. "She knows where you live."

"We'll go to the police station," Megan said. She didn't know if they would be able to help, but at least it might keep them safe for a little while. She glanced in her rearview mirror, waiting for the headlights of a small black car to appear. But the road was windy, and the headlights never showed. What was Sylvia playing at?

"I don't know why she's not following us," Megan said. Fred laid his head between the seats atop the consul, and she rested her hand on his soft fur, stroking him. "It makes me nervous."

"Maybe she knows you won't head home," Crystal shrugged. "Do you think she can track us somehow?"

Megan's mind was racing so fast it made her dizzy. "I don't know," she finally answered, coming up to the police station. "With a million dollars at stake, I imagine she can do quite a lot."

Megan put the car into park just as her phone rang. It was nearing midnight, and she glanced up at Crystal as she answered, placing it on speaker.

"The police won't help you," Sylvia's voice rang out in the small car, and Megan felt Fred's fur bristle.

She rubbed him gently. "And why's that?" Megan asked, glancing back when a black car with its headlights off sped by. Sylvia.

"Because they can't touch me. They wouldn't dare, even if they suspected something. Do you know what a false accusation to someone with diplomatic immunity could mean for them? Small town cops?"

A dry laugh burst through the phone. "They wouldn't stand a chance. Any career in law enforcement would be over."

"And what about Santiago?" Megan asked, catching a look of alarm from Crystal, who gestured toward the police station. "He has enough status behind him to put you away, especially with you stealing authentic pieces out from under him."

"I did no such thing," she spit out. "I was hired to facilitate a trade of merchandise. There's nothing illegal about that. If his company can't be responsible enough to keep track of their valuables, that's not my problem."

"Who hired you?" Megan nodded at Crystal, and they opened their doors, making their way to the police station.

"An old friend of his, of course. Aren't they always the ones? Now tell me, where's the necklace? I have a flight I can't miss and, believe me, if they send in a new agent to take my place, it won't be a good thing for you. I was just going to put Fred to sleep, no suffering involved. I doubt anyone else would be so kind."

"What has he done? Your conflict is with me."

"Exactly," she said, her voice ringing with cruelty. "And what you love becomes the target because it can cause a reaction."

There was a thump behind them, and Megan spun around to see Fred pushing through the door that Crystal had left open. He lengthened his body into a full run and crossed the street, disappearing into the forest.

"Fred!" Megan shouted, racing back to the car. "I'll be there," she shouted into the phone before hanging up.

"What do you mean by that?" Crystal asked. She hadn't moved and stood angled toward the police station.

"I'll tell you later," Megan hopped in the front seat, shouting out the window. "Just get them to come to the airport in one hour!" She pulled out and gunned the engine, heading to where she thought Fred had gone.

When she pulled up to her house, a thousand fears crowded around her. Fears of intruders and spies and syringes. But she needed to find Fred, and she assumed he was simply so eager to get home that he couldn't wait for her. She walked around the house to the deck, but he wasn't there. Something was rustling in the forest, and she walked down the steps, rounding the corner to the side of the house.

Fred was digging furiously against the foundation just as she'd caught him doing before. He was covered in the rich, dark dirt of an evergreen forest. His entire front half was sunk down in his work, which looked to be digging up her house.

"Fred." Megan approached him, stepping back as dirt that flew through the air behind him. "What are you doing? You get kidnapped and race back home to dig a hole? That makes no sense."

With a sigh, she left him to it and pulled her phone out, making a single call to Derek. "Can you meet me at the airport with your former boss?" she asked. There was silence on the other end. "I think I know who caused everything with Santiago. She's an international spy, and she's flying out in less than an hour. Can you make it?"

He agreed and promised to meet her there.

She knelt next to Fred and rested her hand on his back.

He looked up for only a second and then returned to his madness with vigor.

"Ugh." Megan sighed, exhausted. She leaned her back against the house and sat on a soft pile of excavated dirt. Her eyes closed. "She needs the necklace, Fred. The real one. If I had it, I would just give it to her. It would mean you stay safe and she disappears, and I like both of those outcomes. It's worth—" Something landed in her lap, and she jumped. Looking down, she gasped, tapping her finger across the jewelry quickly, counting.

Eighty-four South Sea pearls covered in dirt. She lifted the necklace up, holding it out in front of her. The pearls of Cleopatra. The legend Lyanna had paid two million dollars to have, resting casually in her hands. She turned to Fred. "You ran home from the cliffs before Sylvia could get here and you buried them, didn't you?"

Fred sat, looking solemnly back at her. His eyebrows twitched, and his lip was snagged on one tooth.

He looked guilty.

"What else have you got down there?" Megan set the pearls aside and leaned over the hole. "Fred, you bandit." She laughed, pulling out a pile of crumpled, dirty letters. "This is horrible! You could be prosecuted, you know."

She set the letters aside, prepared to find their owners

later. "And what's this?" She scooped away more dirt from around the corner of a plastic bag with a folded piece of paper inside. It was much older than the letters, and the dirt around it was hardened with age.

"This wasn't from you." She scraped around it, slowly freeing the paper from its place. "This has been down here for years."

Wiggling it free, she lifted it from the dirt. There was a hole on one side of the bag, and she pulled a page of yellowed, aged paper out, unfolding it. The writing was faded, but thankfully it had been written in pen. The beautifully penned cursive spoke to a time in the past.

Dear occupant,

This house has been a protection from the world for me, and so it must be for you. If you find this letter, you have been blessed by the god of the sea, surely. For it won't be easily found. I assume its contents are damaged or lost, but if not, you are the new owner of the necklace of Cleopatra. I bequeath it to you. The pearls are more valuable than most would consider a life to be, so walk your path carefully.

I've chosen you because I trust fate more than man. She is the great equalizer, not to be persuaded or bargained with. And so, she has given this to you. Do not tempt her to punish your behavior from this time forward, I warn. And lastly, enjoy the moments you have with this treasure. Any length of time with these pearls in your possession is a gift that few obtain.

Yours,

Charles

MEGAN'S HEAD SPUN. BUT THERE WAS NO TIME TO TAKE IT in. She had to get to the airport. Now that she had the necklace, she trusted everything would work out smoothly. Soon, there would be no threats against her... and Fred would be safe.

She gathered the letters and tucked them and the necklace in her inside jacket pocket, along with the note and plastic bag. Fred was looking back at her with distaste.

"I know," she said, rubbing his dirt-crusted ear. "It stinks, but we need to keep you safe, right?"

His sour expression didn't change.

With a sigh, she climbed the steps to the deck and took the leash from a hook on the wall. "I won't have you running off." She clipped it to his collar and winked at him. "And just think, I could use it like nunchucks if I have to."

His mouth stayed shut tight, as if refusing to let his tongue loll out and accidentally look pleased with her. In short, he disagreed. She could see it plain as day.

"Okay, I'll admit my nunchuck skills are lacking. I guess it's up to you to save the day, deal?"

He sneezed. The agreement was set.

Chapter Twenty-Two

✦❦✦

The airport was only a few years old and bigger than one would think being so far away from Seattle. But since so many wealthy vacationers enjoyed coming out to the national forests, it had been built to accommodate.

Megan wrapped Fred's leash around her hand and strode through the sliding doors as if it were customary to bring a large, dirt-covered Great Dane everywhere she went. The security guard at the entrance raised his eyebrows but didn't say anything. He seemed a little glazed with sleep, as it was nearing 2 a.m. A red-eye flight for Sylvia.

Within her first few steps inside the building, Crystal appeared at her side.

"Where have you been?" She whispered frantically. "Her flight is almost boarding! And why is Fred all dirty?"

Shaking her head, Megan headed for the escalator. There was only one. "Where are the officers?" she asked. Crystal smiled, glancing around casually. "They're watching her from across the upper level. We were waiting for you, actually."

"Well, I'm waiting for someone—two someones." Megan

scanned the upper level, spotting Derek right off with Mr. Yost stood next to him, and they both appeared to be upset. She supposed giving him the task of working with his former boss might have been a little rude.

"Right over there," Megan whispered, tilting her head.

Crystal's pale blue eyes flickered toward the lawyers. "Okay, who are they?" she asked.

"Never mind." Megan waved them off as they started toward her, and they faltered, coming to a halt and standing awkwardly. "Let's just confront Sylvia and see if we can avoid having to do anything else."

The spy was sitting calmly, wearing black velvet boots and a long, tailored overcoat. She glanced up at the two women as they came closer, smiling as friendly as any stranger would do.

"Can I help you?" she asked, her voice as smooth as it had been at the gala. Megan had adored it when they'd met, but now the enchantment was lost.

She signaled to Sheriff Anderson and Officer Kellen, who were dramatically changing their positions every few seconds and doing a terrible job of being stealthy. One of the flight attendants watched them from the announcement booth and Megan beckoned to her as the officers ambled closer. The flight attendant, who smiled very cheerily for 2 a.m., walked swiftly in her tall navy-blue heels that matched her skirt and jacket. "Yes, miss?" she asked.

Megan turned from the flight attendant to the officers, and then back at Sylvia. "This woman is a criminal. An international spy," she said, "You cannot allow her on the plane."

Next, she turned to the officers. "She must be arrested for animal cruelty, assault, theft, and corporate espionage."

"Excuse me," Sylvia said, "I believe you have mistaken me for someone else."

"Megan," Sheriff Anderson wrapped his arm around her

back and led her a few steps away from the group. "This isn't the way things are done."

Megan turned around, speaking loudly. "This isn't her?" She turned back to the officer. "You told me there was a spy in the area, and this woman has stolen my dog, threatened my life, and attempted to steal a priceless piece of jewelry."

"No," Sheriff Andersen's voice boomed, and conversations around them hushed. Curious passengers began looking on, and the sheriff lowered his voice. "I'm sorry, but I'm going to have to tell you that this is the wrong person."

"Perhaps this will help." Sylvia stood, holding up her passport. "I also have my birth certificate." She fished another paper from her purse. "My name is Anaisha Dhar. I travel here often from India. I'm sorry if you believe I resemble someone else. I assure you that my business here is professional."

The sheriff took the documents, and Megan glanced at them, reading the name and confirming the picture. It was her. Possibly the *real* her.

Crystal crossed her arms, grumbling, "Then she lied to us because this is definitely her." Her gaze was firm and more intimidating than Megan had ever seen, and she felt suddenly guilty for getting her friend so involved in a lie. After all, she knew perfectly well that nothing she did would stop Sylvia from getting on the plane. But then, that wasn't what she was after.

"I do need to begin the boarding process, ma'am," the flight attendant said kindly. She offered a sympathetic smile and returned to her booth, speaking into the microphone. Passengers around them stole glances as they lined up. Sylvia stood as well, giving a tight-lipped smile.

"Good evening," she said, turning slowly and keeping her gaze on Megan before walking away.

"This can't be happening," Crystal said. She glared at the officers. "You're letting her get away."

"No," Megan said, turning around. Mr. Yost and Derek had come forward in the commotion, and Megan eyed Derek severely. "*He* didn't get away."

"What are you talking about?" Derek asked, his beautiful face full of curiosity.

Megan crossed her arms, feeling more confident with each moment that passed. His ease was lessening, and she could see a tinge of moisture along his upper lip.

"You went to school with Santiago, didn't you? Same apartment building that first year. Two doors down."

"I did." He nodded. "That's no secret."

"What I couldn't make sense of this whole time..." Megan shook her head, and tendrils of auburn hair brushed softly against her cheeks. "Was how it all related. It wasn't working. Santiago's clients hired him only recently to find this necklace." She reached her hand into her coat and pulled out the South Sea pearls. "But then, he discovered the fake pieces of jewelry had been carefully traded out for years. One piece at a time. He tells no one, but begins speaking to a lawyer, hoping to search out the culprit. Over the course of another year, this lawyer hires on a young associate. You."

"You're skipping significant portions of my life, Ms. Henny, just to make me look suspicious." Derek's calm had broken, and she could tell he was holding in a healthy amount of anger. But his voice remained smooth.

"Fair enough." Megan nodded. "I thought the same thing, so I looked into your professional past. Turns out, you never graduated but left college the same time that Santiago did without a degree. When Santiago began working in France, traveling for weeks at a time, you mysteriously ended up on vacation only a block away."

"This is ridiculous." Derek threw his hands in the air,

turning to leave. Sheriff Anderson side stepped across his path. "I request that you stay, sir."

Derek glowered. "And?" he grumbled. "She hasn't said anything that incriminates me. Nothing."

"Not yet, but here's the thing." Megan held her hand out, and Mr. Yost dropped a cell phone into her palm.

"Hey!" Derek shouted for the first time. "That's my phone! You stole that! It's my private property!" His voice was aggressive, but he didn't make a move.

Megan was glad for the police officers by her side. She opened the screen and pulled up an app.

"This"—she turned it to the others—"is called a puppet master app. With it, you can spread the app like a virus to other phones, and all data collected comes back to the puppet master. In this case, audio recordings."

"I've never seen that before," Derek growled, although some fight had left his voice.

"There was an identical icon on my phone, Yost's phone, and Santiago confirmed he'd found the app hidden on his phone just before being arrested. Is that correct, Mr. Yost?"

Yost stepped forward, his burly arms crossing over his chest. "That's right. I suspected Derek of spying, but I didn't know how. I believed he only did it to prove Santiago was guilty. He didn't hesitate telling me from the beginning that he didn't trust Mr. Fitch's testimony of the events."

"So, what was it that tipped the scales?" Megan asked. "Here, you had a successful thing going by fabricating pieces you'd seen at Santiago's business and hiring Sylvia to swap them with the originals. As an underground expert in the jewelry trade, she could get you top dollar. Why stop?"

Derek didn't answer, his expression dark and boring back at Megan.

"Santiago called you, didn't he?" Megan said. "He'd seen you during his last trip to France and began looking into your whereabouts. I have his testimony recorded right here." She lifted up her phone.

"He had no proof, that's what really set me off," Derek interrupted, sweat now glistening on his forehead. "Nothing. Just a hunch and here he comes, calling me up and threatening *me*. The only thing I could use was his shaky past with his parents. They were easier to persuade than I thought. Turns out they'd been secretly looking into the fabricated jewelry, unbeknownst to him. They suspected Santiago was the one trading the pieces and taking the profit."

Mr. Yost stepped forward. "So, you swapped your role in the narrative with Santiago. Willing to destroy a family and career to cover your own hide."

The clanking sound of metal against metal had everyone's eyes turning to Sheriff Anderson. He stepped forward with handcuffs in one hand. "I'm going to have to ask you to turn around, sir. We're taking you in for questioning on suspicion of espionage."

"You'll never get any proof of this," Derek threatened, his face twisting with anger.

"Actually, we already have." Officer Kellen held up a document. "Dates, names, emails. Your spy friend, under the alias of Sylvia, slipped these to me when she presented her passport. Turns out, when you work with shady people, they have no problem blackmailing you in exchange for their own freedom."

Derek's mouth dropped open, and his eyes skittered across the script on the page. "She's lying," he said, shaking his head as the sheriff guided him back to the escalator, throwing Megan a wink.

She watched as they stepped onto the escalator and slowly lowered from view.

"You..." Crystal giggled. Megan turned around, and a grin

split across her face. Crystal lifted her arms in the air. "You did it!" she shouted, her voice echoing around them.

"Incredible job, Ms. Henny," Mr. Yost said, offering his hand. "When you told me about the scorpion app, I was able to secure his phone under exigent circumstances. It came together quickly after that."

Megan shook his hand. The relief was so overwhelming that tears stung her eyes, but she blinked them away. "Can I be the one to tell Santiago?" she asked.

"Absolutely."

Fred licked at the pearls in Megan's hand, and she flinched, lifting them up. Her eyes met Crystal's and Mr. Yost's, each one of them in awe.

"So, those are the real thing?" Crystal asked, her voice enchanted.

Megan smoothed her finger along one of the pearls, wiping at the dirt to reveal the glossy gem. "They are."

"Might I ask, Ms. Henny?" Mr. Yost reached out and patted Fred on the top of his head. "If this is the item Santiago's clients were searching for, the legend of Cleopatra's pearls... what do you plan to do with them?"

"Actually, I have a message on my phone from Lyanna, Mr. Dewald's fiancée. Turns out they eloped just yesterday. She said my advice to her was something she couldn't put out of her mind. After days of pondering, she concluded that the universe was speaking to her. And so, she ran off to get married."

Megan gently placed the pearls back in her pocket. "These pearls might just end up in Paris at the Louvre. Their displays of famous fine jewelry are incredible, and I think they'd be very interested in these." She grinned back at her companions as they headed to the entrance together. "And can you imagine Lyanna's reaction when she sees these at the Louvre as a new exhibit on her honeymoon?"

"Incredible," Crystal said, "she'll never doubt again." She linked arms with Megan and sighed. "But what I'm more excited about is the reaction from Santiago when he learns he's completely cleared of all charges."

Megan grinned back at Yost, and he nodded his head. "All right, all right." He pulled out his phone. "Let's not wait around."

AFTER DROPPING CRYSTAL OFF AT HER HOUSE AT NEARLY 5 a.m., Megan pointed her red hatchback toward home. Her little house in the woods still needed so many repairs she wasn't sure where to start. All the commotion the past weeks had kept her from even beginning a sandwich shop, and bills had come due. She wasn't sure how things were going to work out... but at least she had Fred.

Curled up in his favorite spot in the passenger's seat, he'd jumped in as soon as Crystal had vacated it and then promptly fell asleep. She had one hand on his back, enjoying his silky coat and the rise and fall of his breathing.

They pulled up to the house and she turned the car off, sitting in the silence of the woods. It was her favorite place to be, covered by protective pine branches and surrounded with only the noise of the trees. She opened the door and Fred offered a tired gust of breath that flapped his cheeks before following after.

Once inside, she hunkered down on the couch. She was too tired to even move. The thought of washing her face and changing into pajamas was exhausting.

Talking with Santiago had been brief, as he wasn't allowed much time. But his voice had cracked when he'd thanked her, and she couldn't get it out of her head. Soon, he would be done with that place. Found innocent of all charges. Mr. Yost was on his way back to Seattle and said it would only be a matter of days.

Closing her eyes, she fished the necklace out of her pocket and set it on the couch next to her. Next was the bundle of letters. "Okay, Fred." She glanced at him. He opened one eye and then closed it again. "Which neighbors do I need to apologize to?"

But when she rubbed the dirt off of the first letter, her own name was hand-written across the front. She flipped to the next... and the next. "These—Fred, they're all for me."

Fred sat up with a snort, looking at her with tired, droopy eyes. "And they're from *Kenneth*. How long have you been hiding these? What could he..." She picked one letter out of the bunch and turned it over, curious. "Have to say to me?"

She broke the seal and opened a page of paper with a hand-written letter. *My dear Megan*, he began. The date in the upper corner was over three weeks prior. She read through his message quickly and opened the next, written a few days before the previous one. His thoughts were written out carefully, telling her of casual day-to-day events, and then each one ended with his gratitude for meeting her. He told her he thought of her often and he mentioned their kiss, but only once. She organized them by date, realizing the first one arrived only four days after he'd left. And he hadn't missed a week since, sometimes sending them only a few days apart.

The last letter he sent was different from the rest. More mechanical, like there was nothing left to say. Rejected. No wonder he'd been so confusing lately. He thought she'd completely ignored his letters. What was he supposed to think about that?

Megan dropped her head into her hand. "Oh my goodness, Fred." She sighed. "What am I going to tell him? Why are you hiding these?"

He seemed to notice she was speaking to him, and he

stood and joined her at the couch. His nose was smudged with dirt, and his head was tilted down with his eyes looking up at her.

I'm sorry.

She took his face in her hands. "Are you worried he's going to take me away?"

His head lowered to her lap, with his eyes still gazing up at her.

"Hmm," she mused, rubbing under one floppy ear. "Well, don't worry about that. No, sir. You and me, Mr. Fred." She lifted his head and leaned down, looking closely into his eyes. "But having more friends is a good thing, right? More treats, more walks, more scratches. I don't see a losing side for you in this scenario."

He yawned, and after half a second, Megan yawned too.

"Yeah, you're right," she said. "Sleep first. But I'm talking to him tomorrow, Mr." She pointed to him as he curled up on the floor again. Walking to her bedroom, she yelled over her shoulder, "And you're going to apologize!"

Chapter Twenty-Three

※ ❀ ※

The boardwalk had never felt so long. She'd sent Kenneth a text before falling asleep that morning asking to talk to him, and he'd responded with an offer to take her to dinner. But she'd gone and slept until nearly 4 p.m. and now her heart was racing. She felt dead on her feet after spending a frantic hour showering and getting ready. Now she walked with damp hair still drying in the warm breeze, a summer dress and flip-flops, and a rehearsed apology in her head.

She glanced down at the Great Dane trotting gracefully alongside her. "You first," she said, not surprised when he ignored her. He'd been acting a little upset with her all day. "Look, I'm sorry I didn't get up to feed you breakfast. But you still got a late lunch, so in the morning tomorrow it'll be like having two-times the food." She jiggled his collar playfully.

His nose twisted.

Megan chuckled. Then she spotted Kenneth at the end of the boardwalk, and her laughter died in her throat. She slowed, remembering the sweet words of his letters. He met her gaze with a cautious expression, but she doubted he was nearly as nervous as she was. She feared her pulse would have her passing out right in front of him.

"Hi Megan," he said, taking a hesitant step closer. He wrapped one arm around her in a quick hug.

"Hey," she mumbled into his ear before stepping back. He always seemed to smell of musk and amber, but today it made her lightheaded.

He rubbed at the back of his neck with a quick grin. "You needed to talk to me?"

"Yeah." Megan gazed back at him for a moment, trapped in the words of his first letter. *You both terrify and mystify me.*

A seagull called, and she flinched. "Yeah," she repeated. "I believe Fred owes you an apology."

Kenneth tipped his head, looking down at the canine at her feet, who was completely ignoring them while watching a boy throwing a beach ball.

"Fred," Megan said, tugging on his leash. His head whipped around, and he looked up at her. "Do you have something to say?"

His eyes darted to Kenneth and back. With a shaking hand, Megan pulled a bundle of letters from her purse. "He's been digging under the house, and I had no idea he was burying your letters." She swallowed, not able to look up at him again. "I found them yesterday and just read them early this morning."

"Ah." Kenneth sighed.

"I..." Megan took a breath and looked into his deep brown eyes. "I love them. I'm so sorry you never got a response."

He held her gaze, and it melted her heart like butter. But there was more she needed to say. "I would have told you that spending time with you is exhilarating and so fun." She smiled. "I've adored every second."

Her smile faltered. "But there's a lot I wish I could change right now." She stepped closer to him as a group of friends passed by, whispering. "I wish I could change the pain I feel by getting close to someone again. I wish I could trust my feelings completely. I wish there was nothing holding me back."

In his eyes, she saw the discouragement deepen with each piece of her explanation. He reached out slowly, taking her hand.

"But I can't change the pain," she said, "and my feelings are reckless right now, and..." Her eyes watered, and she blinked quickly. "And there's a lot holding me back."

He squeezed her hand. "It's okay," he said quietly. "I wondered how things were going. You told me a little about the engagement, but no more than that. I didn't realize it had been so recent. I'm sorry if I..."

His eyes took in all of her face as he gazed back at her. "If I ever got too close when you maybe just needed time." He glanced down at their hands and back into her eyes. "Do you want to tell me about it? I'm happy to be a listening ear." He gestured to the cafe where the lighting was low; music played and guests chattered.

Fred licked their clasped hands with his big warm tongue, leaving a trail of slobber.

"Eh!" Megan lifted her hand up, laughing. Kenneth laughed with her, giving Fred a good scratch.

"You're forgiven, Fred." He chuckled. "How about the next time I see you, I bring you another tie to chew?"

Megan linked her arm around Kenneth's. "I say we get some dinner. My treat," she said, enjoying the way his arm felt tangled with hers.

They chatted and laughed, leaving the tense moments at the door. Megan for once found herself able to talk openly about her relationship with Jarron, explaining how things had been without getting emotional or even upset. She could see the disapproval in Kenneth's eyes as she explained the way she'd been treated, and she appreciated him for it but didn't require it. Something about sharing that part of her life had her feeling in control of it. Past it. Recovering.

When they ended the evening with only a hug, she couldn't resist kissing his cheek. "Thank you so much," she said. He smiled in a way that had her heart warming. "It was completely my pleasure, Ms. Henny."

They parted with Megan glancing behind her more than once. And more than once, Kenneth was looking back as well.

But she didn't go home. Instead, Megan crossed the parking lot to the rows of food trucks. More had come since she'd last been to the boardwalk, adding a noodle hut and waffle truck. Delicious fragrances came from every direction, making her mouth water even though she wasn't hungry. Fred sniffed with vigor, turning toward the meatiest flavors, like the turkey legs and the teriyaki rice bowls.

At the donuts and tea truck, Margaret waved at her while handing out an order to one of the many customers in line. But Desmond wasn't helping his grandma anymore. Megan passed three more vendors before coming to a small stand with wagons and picnic tables parked alongside it and shade canopies covering the area. A big, hand-printed sign read *Save the Hermit Crabs,* and Desmond was chatting excitedly with a mother and father and their young daughter at one of the tables.

Just as Megan and Fred got closer, the family stood and thanked Desmond, walking off with their new plastic carrier. It had a small layer of sand at the bottom and two spiral shells were brightly painted, with the little hermit crabs inside scuttling back and forth. The father held the container while the young girl jumped up and down alongside him.

She turned back and shouted, "Thank you, Desmond!"

The young teen waved with a content smile on his face. Megan stared at him for a moment. It was such a huge transition to what he was only a week ago. She tried to take it in. Fred sat down and scratched at his ear as if he wasn't impressed.

"Hey," Desmond said, turning to her.

Megan smiled. "Yeah, hey." She laughed. "How's business?"

"Oh man," he gushed, sweeping one hand over the large aquarium that housed dozens of hermit crabs. "It's going great. They're a huge hit! I think people really like that one hundred percent of their donation goes to keeping the beach clean. Sometimes they give me way more than ten dollars."

"That's great, Desmond."

"Thanks to you." He smiled. "If you hadn't talked to the mayor, none of this would be possible. He said he hadn't even noticed the changes on the beach with the hermit crabs and seagulls. He gave me permission to collect up to fifty crabs per day. Said they'd survey the beach at the end of every week, and when things get more in control, we'll just close up shop."

"So, you're not getting paid?" Megan asked. It was a great gesture for him to be so involved in conservation, but he still needed something for his time.

"Ah, about that." His grin widened. "The mayor found a grant for teen sea-life conservation, and it awarded me five grand to use toward my college when I'm ready."

He tucked his hair behind his ears—something she'd never seen him do before. It was nice to see so much of his face. He really was a handsome kid. His eyes brightened.

"Oh! I forgot. He even said we can offer an incentive for everyone who adopts a hermit crab. If they come in September for the Fall Festival and return their crab to the beach, they'll get a one-of-a-kind Seacrest T-shirt."

"That's such an amazing idea," Megan said. "I'm sure a lot

of people will love coming back and setting their hermit crab free."

She smiled, remembering when Desmond left his hair in his face and hardly every spoke. He was practically a different kid. A new family came to browse hermit crabs, gathering around the aquarium.

Desmond gave her a quick wave, heading over to them. "See ya later, Megan."

She waved back. "See ya."

It was a wonderful day, even though she'd slept through most of it. The sun was already beginning to set, chasing its rippled reflection in the calm, evening sea. She started back to the car with Fred. He seemed to walk closer to her now, as if he were anxious, and she hadn't notice him pull on the leash once.

They got in the car, and before starting it, she leaned over the console, rubbing his face in her hands. "Good boy," she said, and his tail *thwapped* at the passenger side door.

"I love you, buddy. Don't worry, no one's taking you away again." He closed his eyes, panting. "Ready to go home?" His tail hit the door a few more times and Megan smiled. "Okay, then. Let's go."

Back at the house, she punched in the code, feeling grateful that Kenneth was so stubborn about getting her a security system. It really did help her feel calmer on her own. She went about her way getting ready to sleep again, even though she'd practically just woken up. Still, she washed her face, changed into her softest leggings, and made a hot cup of herbal tea.

With a sigh, she finally sat down.

Someone rapped on the door and she flinched, nearly spilling the hot liquid onto her lap. "Really?" she muttered, setting her cup aside on the coffee table. Fred leapt up from his spot and raced to the door. In the privacy window, she saw waves of shiny, perfect hair, and a smile grew on her face.

She pulled the door open to see Santiago looking back at her. He wore sweatpants, sneakers, and a T-shirt and held a bundle of white roses. The smile on his face was brilliant, but it couldn't surpass the energy coming from his eyes. They were always stunning. But now, as she caught a tint of moisture gathering there, they blazed with color.

"For you," he whispered, holding the roses out. "Thank you doesn't really seem to cut it, but—"

She took the roses and wrapped her arms around him, leaving him to finish his statement through a curtain of her unruly hair.

"Thank you."

Closing her eyes, she held him tight. He clung to her, the only movement coming from his chest while he breathed, as if her hug was everything he needed. Fred pranced around them, jumping and panting and circling.

"I owe you my career, Megan." He rubbed her back before separating. "My life, maybe. All I can say is thank you. So much."

"Come on." Megan took his hand and brought him inside with her. "I was just going to relax with a hot cup of tea and honey. Want to join me?"

"You have no idea how amazing that sounds." Santiago closed the door behind him, locking up. "I see you've upgraded the security."

"Kenneth did that for me," she said as she pulled a cup from the kitchen cabinet. "He was pretty worried about me way out here on my own. Especially after I'd met with Carter Dewald and Lyanna, and they turned out to be scouring the world for my necklace."

"Wait, that's not how I heard it. You what?"

She turned around to see him gawking, his complexion a

tinge pale. With a wink, she pressed the hot water tap and filled his cup, adding herb bags and a dollop of honey and giving it a quick stir. She handed him the cup.

"Have a seat," she said with a playful grin. The mixture of shock and admiration in his eyes was entertaining. "We've got a lot to catch up on."

*IN BOOK 3, *A TAIL FOR TROUBLE*, HIKING TRAILS ARE IN disrepair and Megan and Fred nearly topple down the mountain. But when Crystal's father goes missing and a little boy too, can Megan connect the dots and solve the mystery? READ NOW.

Also by Rimmy London

Made in United States
North Haven, CT
25 April 2026

10433404R00146